Submit

SUITED FOR SIN: BOOK THREE

ANGEL PAYNE

Copyright © 2018 Waterhouse Press, LLC
Cover Design by Waterhouse Press, LLC
Cover Photographs: Shutterstock

Paperback ISBN: 978-1-64263-116-6

Submit

SUITED FOR SIN: BOOK THREE

ANGEL PAYNE

WATERHOUSE PRESS

Dedicated...as always...every time, all the time, to my wonderful man: my beautiful Thomas. Your support and belief has made so many of my dreams come true. I love you so much!

CHAPTER ONE

"Can stars really collide?"

The question came from the lips, coated with dark-red lipstick, of Dante Tieri's date for the evening. Her name was Suzanne Collier—*Suzanne*, not "Suz" or "Suzie," she was sure to tell him—and the question was actually refreshing. It was the first thing she'd said all night that didn't involve his clothes, his business, or his new condo at the Elysian, as well as the tour she clearly expected at the end of the night. In short, she was one of his usual date selections. Blonde, beautiful, young, vivacious, but close enough to his forty-three that nobody cocked a brow. The checklist went on from there, and nearly all the boxes were filled. To all who cared, he'd made an ideal selection for one of the most important Chicago events he bankrolled each year.

Which made his yawn, concealed as he reached for more champagne, *not* an encouraging thing.

"I'm not sure Elton John was thinking about cosmic physics when he wrote the song, darling." He smiled, amused at gazing into her kohl-caked eyes and facing the cloudy effects of the alcohol. Maybe she'd be more interesting after he got a few more flutes into her. "It's a great lyric, though. One of my—"

Suzanne stole the last word off his lips by smashing hers to them. It was a kiss of determination, enforced by her hand at his nape, gripping him hard. Instinct compelled him to hold her waist as she went for tongue play, though he guessed the

Taittinger had dulled his blood. His body reacted with a mild surge of warmth, nothing more. He opened a little wider, letting her explore him, groaning as she dived for his tonsils with nearly professional confidence.

He did a mental pullback. Shit. She really did kiss like a pro.

He yanked back physically too.

"Thank you," he managed to murmur. "But, umm, appearances, darling." He gazed across the room, through the forest of military dress attire, knowing damn well that none of these people cared who the hell he was or whether he humped an ostrich in front of them. "I'm sure you understand."

"Certainly." Suzanne's reply matched the smooth line she ran down his sleeve with a dark-red fingernail. "Just wanted you to have a preview for later."

He started running a list of I've-gotta-call-it-an-early-night excuses.

His effort was interrupted by a whoop from the dance floor that sliced the air as the ballad ended. The outburst was so loud, it visibly shook the banner overhead.

THANK YOU, CHICAGO VETERANS, ACTIVE DUTY, AND FAMILIES.

As the disc jockey hit the Play button on a bass-heavy dance tune, Dante joined the rest of the crowd to observe his best friend, Mark Moore, sweeping a curvy brunette off her feet. The man's grin was brilliant against his well-trimmed beard as he twirled her a couple of times and then set her down and grabbed her hand, setting a path back to where Dante sat with Suzanne.

Dante greeted the couple with a smirk he had to paste

to his lips. Their giddy delight in each other was so palpable, it made his embrace with Suzanne seem a cartoon. His chest went taut. *Fuck. Just admit it, you asshole. You envy him. More than a little. It's ugly as hell, but it's the truth.*

"Well, Rose." He managed to fake his way through an easy drawl at least, addressing the gorgeous woman nestled against his friend's chest. "Marker Man doesn't raise the roof like that unless there's a damn good reason. And I have a feeling his 'damn good reason' means I'm about to lose a tremendous employee." He arched his brows at Mark. "You talked her into it after all, eh? You put a ring on her finger just two months ago, and now you want her around on a full-time basis? This is the thanks I get for footing the bill on your annual love child of a pet project?"

"Bite me, Tieri." Mark chuckled. "The marines were half my life. And didn't you just sign the contract to bankroll the Memorial Day cruise on the lake too? I think somebody just likes ogling women in uniform."

Suzanne grabbed his elbow. "I could get a uniform."

He was able to ignore her, thanks to Rose Fabian-Moore's musical laugh. "Mr. Tieri, you could turn that gift for flattery into a new business. I'm not *that* huge of a loss. You have some amazing consultants on the Baghdad project."

He grunted. "None who've cared more about getting that school rebuilt, Rose."

The classic angles of her face crunched with emotion. "Yes. I'll really miss those kids." She glanced up at Mark. "Maybe we could take just one more quick trip there, to say good—"

"No." His friend nearly snarled the word. Dante furrowed the brows he'd just hiked at the man. He knew about Mark's

9

intensity; hell, he shared the trait to many degrees. But he'd never seen Marker Man this ferocious. "No," Mark repeated. "And that's final. Baghdad is no place for a pregnant woman."

Shock froze him for a second. Then he surged off the stool. "What. The. Fuck? You spunky dog!" He yanked his friend into a hug. "No wonder you hollered like a teenager. Congrats, man."

"Thanks." Mark said it with heavy meaning. "That means a lot, Inferno Boy."

Though he chuckled at the nickname, Dante had to turn his gaze away again, lest Mark see what was going on in his soul. The self-honesty that had propelled him to millionaire status now turned traitor, forcing him to recognize that his envy had mutated to jealousy.

Goddamn it, there was no denying it. He craved what Mark had found. The connection. The need. Yeah, even the protective snarls. He longed for the magic his friend had been brave enough to go after with all emotional guns blasting, despite the silly social whispers that had followed. Mark and Rose shared something that drowned it all out anyhow. Their love played a symphony of its own, blasting away those small minds and their meaningless squeals of disapproval. The two of them were certainly none the worse for wear in getting deleted from half the social invitation lists in the city. To be frank, they seemed happier for it.

Hell. He could really get used to a calendar like that.

"Umm...Mr. Tieri? Are you busy?"

The shy greeting, coming from just out of his periphery, forced Dante to turn back. A female navy officer now stood there, a lieutenant if he read the stripes on her shoulder accurately, who looked ready to bolt from nervousness. He smiled out of sheer sympathy for the petite redhead. She was bracketed by two friends. A blonde, equally tiny, joined her in the squirming act. The last member of the trio, a taller brunette, stood off to the side and rolled her eyes in the universal code for *get me out of here right now*. His gaze was pulled to her. He got this reaction from a lot of people and prided himself in easing it by turning on the old-world Italian charm he'd learned so well from the source of the stuff: his grandfather. He tilted a big grin and—

It froze. *He* froze.

The halt to his gut, his chest, and his rational thinking happened sometime just after the rest of his senses fell ass over elbows into the magic of looking at her. Her sable hair was pulled back into a typical naval bun, now seeming more a goddess's knot on her head. Her dramatic brows swept over forest-deep eyes. Her mouth was a generous sweep of dark cherry, the bottom a bit fuller than the top. Her nose wasn't perfect, thank God, with a slight rounded tip that seemed made for kissing. Her strong chin perfectly finished the heart shape of her face.

His gaze dipped, taking in the rest of her. God save him, he couldn't help it. She was slim yet curved in all the right places. Her breasts looked gentle and plush, decent handfuls that were matched by the soft swell of her ass, and legs that made her government pumps look as erotic as pole-dancer stilts. Damn it, when had naval skirt suits gotten so sexy?

He told himself to shake it off. To crack some lame one-liner that would set her at ease and make her want to stay here, in his direct universe, nearly close enough to touch. Shit, just thinking of *touching* her—well, now he knew what creative visualization meant, didn't he? As well as sweet torture.

As well as complete irony.

Three minutes ago, he'd tossed a symbolic coin into the fountain of fate. He'd waved his goddamn melodramatic mental flag, declaring cravings for connection and need, possessiveness to the point of going feral about it, a lover and not just a date.

Something a lot like this.

In the back of his mind, he heard fate giggling at him. Hysterically.

CHAPTER TWO

She'd been at this "Yay for the Troops" dance party thing for an hour and a half. In Celina Kouris's mind, that was sixty minutes too long. How she let Eve and Reiley talk her in to this was still a mystery, but finally her friends were ready to head out. They were just a dozen steps from the doors when both Eve and Rei stopped and hyperventilated like a discount shoe rack had been dropped in the middle of the Hilton's ballroom. Only this was worse.

The reason for their change in course was a man. Not just any man, she learned as they dragged her to the massive bottom-lit bar in the middle of the room, but the bazillionaire whose credit line had made this spectacle possible. For some reason, Eve thought that required her to approach the guy as if he were the Pope. And to nearly genuflect when he turned, his black designer suit moving easily with him, his megawatt smile a direct contrast to his black, close-trimmed beard.

"Holy shit." Reiley leaned close to Celina as she whispered it. "He's more gorgeous in person! Look at his hair. Holy God, it's doing that curling-around-the-ears thing. You think he'd kill me if I touched it? It's like...like black satin!"

Celina arched both brows. "Girl, you are a commissioned officer of the US Navy Judge Advocate General's Corps. Do *not* tell me you just compared a man's hair to something they make into bad prom dresses."

"Sure did." Reiley giggled. "Deal with it, *girl.*"

The man now kicked his grin at Eve. "Please call me Dante." All too quickly, his gaze swung and locked on *her*. "And no, I'm not busy."

"Dante?" She poured more derision into her tone, using it to counter his unnerving stare. She dared a fast glare back but regretted it at once. She'd relent on one aspect of the man. His eyes were haunting. Did they have *any* color? Did he *ever* blink? She looked closer, drawn by the need to find out. "Is he serious?" she finally managed to quip.

"Completely." Rei kept up her eager whisper. "The name's been in his family for centuries."

"You don't say." Her snort seemed to register on Pope-Man Tieri's radar, but she wasn't surprised. He still didn't stop examining her. Self-consciousness dug in, especially because his date now noticed the same thing. Of course, *she* looked like a magazine ad too, coiffed and cultured, a walking version of the society page. The observation was oddly unnerving.

She shook her head. The loud music had obviously popped a bunch of her mental screws loose. Every time she went to court, she faced men more confident and swaggering than him. And she put them all right back in their place too. She just had to find her game face. Where'd the damn thing gone?

"So what can I do for you ladies?" Tieri asked. "Is there a problem with anything?"

Eve and Reiley laughed with manic energy she'd never seen from them before. "No, nothing at all!" Eve blurted. "We just saw you here and...wanted to say thank you for the party." She bit her lip like an awkward teen. "I'm—errrmmm—oh shit, who am I?"

Tieri turned a little more, his black suit jacket opening to reveal a physique that really could've come from the same beautiful-people magazine as his date. The guy literally bulged in all the right places, which got highlighted even more as he rose from his bar stool with the fluid grace of a dancer. With a slight smirk, he leaned and read Eve's name badge. "Does Pascal ring a bell?"

"Oh yeah! Th-Thank you. Pascal, that's it. Lieutenant Eve Pascal, sir. And these are my friends, Lieutenants Reiley Young and Celina Kouris. We're with the Midwest JAG office."

"Hmmm. Gorgeous *and* smart. Thank you for your service to our country, counselors. This is the least I can do to signify the gratitude."

"The least?" Eve giggled again. "Are you kidding? This party is—well—wow. Seriously. I've been coming since you started it."

"Me too!" Reiley arced her hand in a fast wave.

The man tilted his head, looking to Celina again. His smile hitched at one side. "And you three?"

"No."

She couldn't get it out fast enough. As she shifted her weight, a rush of heat tormented her. His gaze was like a damn spotlight, and she had nowhere to hide. She drew in a breath against the panic that followed. Maybe this was how it started. Maybe this was the opening tactic with men like him. Men who thought their black Amex and their practiced stare could get a woman to drop everything in her life, *everyone* in her life, to float away with them into the sunset on a fifty-foot yacht. Playing to women like her own mother and sister-in-law, who proved them completely right.

"No," she repeated, more firmly this time. "I don't do dances." *Especially ones backed by players like you, Mr. Tieri.*

"Cel!" Rei gave her a playful swat on the arm, but her eyes

were wide with threat. "Be. Nice!"

She flashed a grin of false sweetness. Reiley's reaction ensured she'd gone for exactly the right tone and achieved it.

But her private celebration was destroyed by Tieri's smooth interjection. "It's okay. I don't usually do dances either. I'm just the guy with the checkbook." He nodded to a man who sat nearby, whom Cel only now recognized. It was Mark Moore, former Indiana senator and new Chi-town transplant, looking relaxed and happy as he cuddled with a mahogany-haired woman who looked a lot more normal than Ms. Society Page. "My best friend Mark," he said in introduction. "And the bastard you have to officially thank for this thing. He's just found out he's going to be a daddy. And since his first offspring is currently blowing up the net with her single being downloaded, we need to make sure the next gets a decent round of celebration. Would you ladies care to join us in some more champagne? And of course, one glass of cider for Rose over there."

Again, the man's words included Eve and Rei, but his stare twined only around her. She risked looking directly back this time. And regretted it. He gazed with more determination than ever, as if she were a knot he longed to untangle. And she felt his energy too, pulling at the tight ends of her composure, a relentless tug at her blood, her bones, her nerves...

No. *No.*

The resolve was easy to maintain. All she had to do was remember the house, heavy with Dad's agony, the morning after Mom left them for the president of her bank. And Dylan, the rock of their family, crumbling to emotional dust when Natalie divorced him for an international commodities czar.

She wasn't biting into the same poisoned apple. Or

drinking a drop of the champagne that precluded it either.

"Cel?" It was Eve this time with the big bug eyes, only hers were filled with desperation. "C'mon. You wanna?"

She gave her friend a rueful glance and then steeled her jaw. "I'm sorry. I don't do bubbles either."

"Cel-eeeee-naaaa..."

Now she actually laughed. "God, you're persistent. Listen, you two stay and have fun." She found a spot on the wall that was suddenly interesting. She wouldn't look at him again. She couldn't. "I just need to get out of here. I'll be around the corner, at the Blue Sax Grill. It's safe. See you in a bit."

CHAPTER THREE

An hour later, Dante looked at his watch again. Then rolled his shoulders again. Both actions did nothing to slough the tension that set on him like a vulture from the second his little surprise from fate had walked out the door. He'd watched every step she took on those goddamn gorgeous pumps, inwardly cursing himself for an idiot as she'd left. Every instinct in his body had screamed at him that stars really did collide, that he'd just been handed the fucking proof on life's golden platter, and now he'd let that evidence walk out the door on him.

She'd left, he was certain, *because* of him.

Now things were developing into an even bigger mess.

His scowl literally hurt while he watched Lieutenants Pascal and Young bop by on the dance floor as the middle links of a conga line, fueled by three glasses of champagne apiece. Those were the drinks *he'd* witnessed them suck down. He wasn't sure what other libations had gone into those girls since they'd headed to the dance floor with a pair of dashing young ensigns, but from the looks of it, they were experimenting in the neighborhood of the let's-mix-our-alcohol-and-see-what-happens category now.

With their friend, none the wiser, waiting at a bar around the corner.

Just as midnight struck.

"Shit."

Celina Kouris was a smart woman. That part was clear.

He nodded, needing the move as backup for the reassurance. She was smart, and she also clearly had her friends figured out. She'd eventually discern what was happening and come back to the ballroom.

Wouldn't she?

She hadn't been able to get out of here fast enough. The certainty of it was a nail in his brain. Something about him acted like a single-pole magnet on her, repelling her despite all the signs she gave of wanting to come closer, of wanting to stay. But in the end, when she left, the move was final.

No, she wouldn't come back.

So had she stayed at the Grill?

And if not, where the hell was she now?

"Shit."

A tight sigh next to him wasn't much help. "That's about the twentieth time you've said that, honey."

Suzanne's voice was still smooth as her Botox-injected skin. Dante swung a glance at her. "You're right." He didn't relax, though she curved an anticipating smile. "You want to leave, don't you?" As she drew breath for a flirty return, he pressed a soft kiss to her forehead. At the same time, he beckoned his driver forward with a tick of his fingers. "Vincent will make sure you get home safely, darling. Thank you for your company tonight. I'll call—"

The woman pressed a finger to his lips. "No you won't, Dante." For the first time tonight, real emotion entered her face. "It's okay. Really." She reached inside his jacket pocket and slid out his cell. "Call your damsel in distress, Prince Charming. I'm sure the Blue Sax is easy enough for directory assistance, even during the witching hour."

He gave her a soft smile. He joined another kiss to it, this time to her cheek, as he waited through the four interminable rings it took for the information operator to pick up. With every number he pressed to click through to the Blue Sax, his anxiety ratcheted higher. Christ; he had no idea why, either. This was crazy, like one of those metaphysical premonitions the late-night TV psychics were always having. He knew the woman was named after a Pleiades star and had the eyes of a forest nymph. End of story. It wasn't like her chi could call to his aura, sending messages clear up the street like—

"Blue Sax!" It was a scream more than an answer, given by some kid who couldn't be more than twenty-three.

"Hello?" He didn't hide the confusion in his tone. Like the other end could even hear him. Within seconds, a riot filled his ear. Crashing glass. Splintering wood. Flesh pounding on flesh. At least a dozen voices shouting different versions of the *F* bomb.

"Hello?" the kid shrieked again. "Is...is this the police? Shit, if you can hear me, please come now! Two guys decided to knock heads over some bitch, and now the whole place is going insane. It's like a fucking *Dirty Harry* movie in here! We need—"

He barely took the time to click the line off before tearing out of the Hilton like the building had caught fire. Flames were almost what he expected to find as he whipped his gaze one way and then the other down the block. Providing just as clear as a signal blaze was the melee on the sidewalk fifty yards down, starring a handful of brawlers bathed in aqua-blue light, who lunged at one another like rabid wolves after raw meat.

Dante broke into a sprint. He was glad he did, because he reached the front door half a second before a fleet of Chicago police cars arrived and screeched into a fantail pattern, closing off access to the Blue Sax from anyone else.

Inside, the dim lighting and the flying bodies created a war zone. The two behemoths who'd likely started the brawl now stood on opposing tables, shouting at each other in drunken slurs. Even if they made sense, it was likely nobody heard them over the screeches from the woman who stood at ground level between them, her black hair matted, fake eyelashes drooping with her distraught tears.

"Jesus," Dante muttered. He took in a breath without trying to smell the air and grimaced when he was unsuccessful. It smelled like a dirty locker room drenched in beer. Probably a fitting impression, anyway.

He lunged on, dodging a couple of flying bottles before warding off a couple of bloodthirsty guys with the force of his glare. "Fuck," he growled. A gentleman's act wasn't going to cut it here. Time to go as primal as the rest of this mob. He let loose a full bellow.

"Celina! Celina, are you still here?"

Some poor jerk got thrown down the length of the bar at that second, hollering and smashing glasses as he went. That should have made it impossible for him to hear the moan, full of a female's pain, that came from the stockroom at the back of the bar.

It *should* have, but it didn't.

His senses sharpened with that surreal pull again, that feeling he'd gotten as soon as they'd met, and then again when he'd called here searching for her. He knew, with furious certainty, the moan had been hers.

"Shit!"

He crunched and slid through broken glass and spilled booze as he ran for the stockroom. He slammed the door back, temporarily blinded by the bright light, and then—

"Fuck!"

She'd been pulled back into a corner by two huge guys in black T-shirts and jeans. They pinned her against the wall, one on each side, and had apparently just done so if the full bottle of Jack Daniel's in her right hand was any clear sign. Her hair had tumbled from its pins, and her whole face was racked with fury, except if someone knew to look right into her eyes. Those deep-green depths showed nothing but black now, betraying the terror she barely contained beneath that wildcat's grimace. Dante swallowed hard, hoping like hell that the third hulk in the room, the one now approaching her flailing legs with a couple of lengths of twine, didn't see the same thing.

Hell. The fuckwad noticed, all right. He told her so too, in every inch of his oily grin and every note of his lusty chuckle.

Dante took in her eyes once again, and the dark desperation of them reached out, clouding the edges of his own vision. The haze thickened as his rage did. "Take one step farther, and your dick is going to become best friends with that twine."

The guy flashed a smarmy smile. "Oh yeah, fancy pants? Says you and what army?"

"Army?"

For a split second, he had trouble comprehending that the ferocious sound had come from Celina. But he stared with a gape mixed of pride and shock as she backed it with a move clearly powered by her wrath. Using the beefy arms of her two captors as anchors, she swung her legs up and out. With one decisive kick of her miracle pumps, she caught Smarmy Smile in the center of his crotch. "That's courtesy of the United States *Navy,* asshole. Don't mix us up again."

Dante didn't need another invitation to move. As the bastard doubled over on a groan, he ripped away the twine and whipped a fast figure eight around the guy's thick wrists. He looped the second length of the thick rope through the middle of that bond and then joined the ends and pulled them down, beneath the asswipe's belt line, and grabbed for whatever he could get in one lunge. From the high-pitched squeal he got in reaction, he knew he'd gotten enough. He cinched the bundle tight and then increased the torture by doubling the twine back on itself and finishing with another figure-eight knot.

Smarmy's screams went instantly Dolby stereo in the small room, but they didn't drown the clunks of thick glass meeting a couple of skulls. Despite the rage dominating his blood, Dante grinned. Sure enough, when he looked up, Celina was standing over one of the thugs, the whiskey bottle in both her hands like a baseball bat. The guy on the ground had gone full fetal, one hand clutching his crotch, the other gripping his black-and-blue jaw. The second thug raised his own arms at Celina in surrender, just before he whirled and sped from the room.

Her breath coming in heaves, her eyes still black with terror, she backed toward Dante. He saw the shivers start already, her system revolting from its nuclear blast of adrenaline. Her arms went slack. Her face looked lost. The bottle slipped from her hand and hit the bully under her in his gut.

She took two steps toward Dante. Then fell into his arms.

He'd never felt anything more right.

"I've got you." He murmured it into her ear, never meaning three words more in his life. He tucked her into the crook of his arm. "Can you walk?" When she nodded, the movement strong and steady, he smiled and pressed his lips to her forehead. "Good, because we need to move fast. Out the back. The cops have swarmed the front like flies on shit."

The back alley kicked them out onto Wabash, where he easily hailed a cab and then let Celina give the driver her address.

She had a little house in a pretty section of Arlington Heights, decorated in all the colors he expected. Soft shades of cream, burgundy, and brown were complemented by sturdy pieces in the craftsman style. Her only indulgence in knickknacks was a large collection of photos in frames of various sizes, most depicting the same trio of men who all looked too much like her to be anything but brothers, along with several of a young girl around nine or ten years old. Other framed items included her law degree from Loyola and a flag in a triangle box with a name on the frame plate: Nikias Kouris.

"My grandfather," she explained. "He was a pilot in 'Nam. One of the first grads of the TOPGUN program, though he still got shot down over the wrong lines, saving someone else's bacon. They never found him."

Dante pivoted his attention from the flag, looking down at her. She'd only turned on one light in the room, and now her face was bathed in soft gold light. Shit, she seemed even more a goddess now, mighty yet so damn beautiful.

He swallowed. And told himself to take a step back. Instead, noticing one of her hairpins jutting from a spot near her nape, he leaned in and freed it. He was close enough now to hear her shaky little breath of reaction. So much for moving back. Even an inch would feel too far now.

He held up the pin between them. Swallowed again. If he spoke now, he knew what it would sound like. A man entranced.

A man aroused. He opened his mouth anyway.

"So you come from a long line of ass-kicking heroes."

She laughed at that. Actually, truly laughed. His senses rejoiced in the husky sound of it.

"Something like that," she said and lifted her gaze to fully meet his. The forests were alive in her eyes again, though their depths now danced with something new. The verb itself was new. Yes, her stare *danced* for him. It moved and flowed across his face, as if rewriting the label she'd originally attached to him back at the party.

He scooted closer to her. Like his muscles were going to let him do anything else. "That's pretty damn cool."

The laugh softened to a smile. "Is that so?"

"Yeah." He didn't smile back. Clearly she wrote his words off as smooth-talking bullshit. "It really *is*, Celina."

"All right, all right." She held up both hands, snatching the hairpin from him and tossing it into a bowl with about fifteen others. "I believe you, fancy pants."

He did a double take. She deliberately used the same nickname on him as the dick wad from the Blue Sax—again, an attempt on her part to lighten him up somehow. Dante didn't back off. He didn't feel so "light" right now, and he was damn determined she saw the same thing as he leaned forward, bringing their noses within inches of each other. "You didn't like me very much when we met, did you?"

Her nostrils flared a little. But that was it in the way of tangible reaction. "Very observant, Mr. Tieri."

"Anyone with a pulse would have noticed it, Lieutenant Kouris."

She hitched a little shrug. "Let's just say I usually don't have a lot of patience for cavalier cash-tossers."

Now he stepped back. Well, hell. That was one for the gut—in a breath-halting, not so fucking great kind of way. His jugular felt the force of it too, constricting as he brushed back by another foot.

"Wow. That one's new. I have to admit, I've been prejudged as a lot of different things, but *cavalier cash-tosser*? Hmm. That brings the game to a new low." His mounting anger made his movements jerky as he yanked out his cell phone. "Sorry I'm still dirtying up your house here, Lieutenant. Just let me get Vincent on the line, and I'll be out of your hair. Yeah, I have a driver. Sorry, but sometimes they come in handy for us cash-tossers."

"*Stop.*" With reflexes that shocked him, she snatched the phone from his hand. "I'm going to add 'shitty listeners' to the list too. Did you hear me? I said I *usually* don't have patience for—"

"For what? People like me? Or just guys like me? I'm wealthy, Celina. So what? I also have earlobes that are way too long, an unnatural obsession with Christmas, and I snore the roof off my bedroom." He grabbed the phone back. "But I've also worked hard for my money, so if I want to toss it around a little, then that's my fucking prerogative."

Without taking his eyes off her, he punched in the speed dial for Vincent and the car. He remembered the moment, just hours ago, that he'd beheld her for the first time. He'd picked up on her discomfort. He'd pegged *her* as a certain kind of person too. A person who would be willing to put away her initial impressions and would get to know what he was really like and perhaps even like the person he was. But her dig—he was right. It was low. And it hinted at a mental wall against his status that ran miles high around her mind.

Her little wince almost did make him stop. But he didn't. Not even when she glared at him and demanded, "Hang it up."

"V? Yo, man, you get Suzanne squared away? Thanks. Listen, I'm in Arlington Heights. The address is—"

He thought he was ready for her little lightning moves now. But the woman had the phone out of his hand, into hers, and at her ear with a move that made even her first frog tongue of a move seem slow. "He's just kidding," she told Vince. "Thanks for your time."

In one move, she punched End Call and hurled the thing across the room, onto the couch.

Dante looked at her and, goddammit, actually fumed. "What the fu—"

"Are you going to listen to me now?"

He snorted. "Why? What good will—"

For the second time tonight, he was cut off from speaking by a kiss. But unlike Suzanne's embrace at the party, this interruption brought a cavalcade of sensation with it. An avalanche of sensations, violent and wonderful, incongruent to the soft, sweet, seeking lips that had brought it all with them. Celina's lips. A mouth, he now realized, he'd been fantasizing about all night.

When her hand slipped up around his neck, he was officially buried by the slide. Suffocated. Cut off from the rest of reality. Lost.

As he pushed open her mouth with his, claiming her with every inch of his tongue and teeth, he prayed they didn't find him for at least a week.

CHAPTER FOUR

Have you lost your damn mind?

Celina would've laughed at the irony of that, if she were certain her mind was responsible for the message. But this man made it impossible to access anything resembling logic. He'd ruined everything from the moment he stared at her at the party, hacking into her psyche with his gaze, gutting her like a black steel knife. She'd even tried to escape, but look where that effort got her. He'd come barging back into her world with damn movie-hero timing, a knight in Armani, his bigger-than-life presence filling the storage room where those three jerks had nearly given her a reason to write off men for the rest of her life. Not that she hadn't considered doing so before.

Oh yeah. That made complete sense *now*, didn't it?

Now, she didn't feel so sensible. Not at all. Actually, she hadn't felt right-side up since she stepped through her own front door ten minutes ago and realized even these familiar walls and furnishings were transformed by Dante's presence. All of it was more vibrant, yet none of it mattered at all. She barely cared about anything in the room, yet she was painfully aware of everything, especially him in it. Filling it. Electrifying it. Consuming it.

And she'd liked it.

Too damn much.

So she'd gone and thrown up her wall of sarcasm. He'd thrown back a volley of indignation. The phone had come out.

The driver got hailed. And that was what she'd wanted, right? It was the perfect solution. He'd be gone and he'd be pissed, guaranteeing his eyes, his body, and his whole dark-knight magic would never tangle up her life again.

Then why did *this* feel like what she wanted instead? Why did his lips feel like heaven and taste like sin, making her crave both at once? Why did his tongue tempt hers into a hot, thrusting dance she couldn't resist, twirling heat through every inch of her body, ending in a liquid pool right between her thighs? Why did his deep, rough groan coax a sigh from her that could only qualify as open, needy, lusty? She didn't do needy! She sure as crap didn't do lusty.

He turned her into a liar on both accounts when he finally pulled away and she twined her grip into his hair to keep him close. Shit, his hair. Turned out "satin" was a damn good descriptor after all. Her action thickened his breathing. His hands bunched against her uniform at the small of her back. His biceps went taut, as if he held himself back from letting them do other things. *Oh God...those other things.* Celina's mind filled with exactly what she wanted those things to be as his rugged beauty consumed her stare. What would those long fingers feel like on her backside...traveling up her thighs... hitching into her panties...and then...

"Oh!" She gasped it, trying to fight off the next part of the fantasy. "Oh, hell!"

To her shock, Dante emitted a grim laugh. "Uh-huh. Welcome to the party."

"Wh-What?"

He dipped his head a little, his ink-dark eyes boring into her. "It's how I've felt all night, *stellina mia.* I've been in hell just thinking about holding you like this. Fighting it like a madman."

Surprise made her jerk back a little. "R-Really?"

His lips quirked. "Yes, really!" She could've sworn he'd break into a chuckle if it wasn't for his tightening grip at her waist and the darkening shadows in his gaze. "Why do you think I was at the Blue Sax?"

She blinked. "I guess—I assumed that Eve and Rei had asked you—"

"No, no. I couldn't stop thinking about *you*. I got worried, and I called. When I heard the place sounding like the apocalypse hit it..." His jaw hardened. "I wasn't a pretty sight."

More shock set in as she began to put pieces together. She'd been so grateful to see him at the Blue Sax, she'd not really thought about why he'd gone there. "You left the party because of that?"

"Because of *you*." Frustration edged his voice, but the next second he stripped it back, giving her a raw rasp. "Celina..."

He huffed but cut himself short on that too. Finally, he leaned in and just kissed her again. Okay, she wasn't sure the man could ever give "just" a kiss, but this touch was different than the plunge he'd gone for after she'd first leaped at him. This was a tenuous press, seeking her reaction, a question without words. But when Celina moaned, tangling her fingers deeper into his hair, it was clear he considered her answer rendered. He opened her, spreading her jaw wide with his, and then dived and claimed and consumed, taking everything save her breath. And she gave it all too. Willingly—even wantonly.

What was going on here? What the hell was he doing to her? She did wanton even less than lusty.

Desire curled through her. She recognized that much. But this version of it—she could only label it as fire. Penetrating, terrifying, consuming fire. It turned her into somebody she didn't recognize. This person looked like her, sounded like her, moved in her skin, but was guided by a new puppeteer tonight. A master with eyes of obsidian, a touch of pure heat, and a claim he'd staked from the second he'd laid eyes on her. A possession he sealed yet deeper by charging into that bar for her tonight.

On his own.

She shifted back for a second, looking at him again. Yet in so many ways, she looked at him for the first time. For a bizarre miracle of a moment, he wasn't "the guy with the checkbook," the stud from the society page, or the CEO playboy with the babe-ilicious arm candy. He was simply a beautiful man who'd bowled her over at a party and, incredibly, felt the same thing for her in return. He was a gift for this night, a blessing of chemistry, a chance to have a fantasy satyr in her bed, taking her in ways she'd only shared with her vibrator before now. This didn't mean he was going to be forever. That word, if she gave it to anyone at all, would go into the hands of someone safe, likely a guy from the base who'd be loyal, steady, sweet, and all about the ten-minutes-foreplay/ten-minutes-screwing plan.

Tonight was *not* about plans.

Though as she gazed deeper into this man's face, looming closer to hers yet again, Celina knew she wasn't going to have much choice on that subject. In response, she could only manage one word.

"Please."

She didn't have to explain. Dante's face shifted, his black brows lowering, his eyes intensifying, his jaw hardening to new angles. He got it. She knew he would. Want was now need. Desire was now fire. Explanations? Done. Thought? *No.* She gave him the plea in the half second before he claimed her mouth with his again. *No more thought. Take it all. Take it from me. Take whatever you want, however you want it. Be my fantasy. Consume me.*

He broke off the kiss only to trail his hot, wet lips to her chin, along her jaw, around her ear, and clear to the back of her neck. When he licked there, it felt like he'd hit her secret candy filling. Sweet warmth drenched her body. She clutched his shoulders and cried out.

"Shhiiiit! Oh!"

Dante gave a tentative hum and then sank his teeth into the same spot.

She screamed.

He growled. "Does that make you wet, *stellina*?"

"Wh-What?" Astonishment spiked her voice.

"You heard me. Answer the question." He did it again, biting harder.

She surged against him, wondering if her skin was going to burst open from the pleasure. "Yes!" she exclaimed. "All right; yes, it's making me wet!"

He swung his head to the other side, sucking her in the exact same spot, now digging one hand into her hair in a fevered search for her hairpins. Through the haze of her senses, she heard the pins hitting the wall, the lamp, the furniture as he hurled them away. When her hair finally tumbled free against her shoulders, he pulled back and stared, his eyes as sharp as switchblades on a moonless night.

"Goddamn it." He spoke it from locked teeth. "You're so beautiful."

The reverence in his tone was like a physical caress. Oh, how easy it would be to believe the feeling in that soft baritone, to think this really meant something to him, to actually open that emotional shell at which he tapped. *No way.* Not happening. The words that ached for release would stay locked in her psyche.

Beautiful? Look who's talking! I want to look at you all night, Dante Tieri. I want to fly in the dark skies of your eyes and cling to the forest of your hair. I want to explore every curve of your lips, feel the rasp of each hair in your beard. I want to get lost in you; would that be okay?

Instead, without a word, she slid fingers up to the first button of his luxurious white shirt and slipped it free. A pulse jumped beneath his beard. His dark gaze never left her. She pulled the next button out and then the next. A sigh bloomed in her throat but hitched as she parted the fabric to reveal the deep bronze of his chest. She pressed her fingers there, wondering if his taut, muscled skin was as hot as his gaze and his kisses.

The second she made contact, a harsh noise burst past his lips. He ripped off the rest of the shirt himself, buttons flying as he surged forward and captured her lips again. But this time, he didn't stop his momentum. Celina stumbled back, erupting with a mewl as she gave in to his assault, until he caught her without a break in the kiss or his stride. Her breath left her as he rammed her against the wall. She came off the floor with his action, and her pumps fell free. Dante still didn't stop, plunging over and over into her mouth as he fitted the juncture of her thighs perfectly along the ridge now bulging in his. He ground their bodies together like two waves of kerosene, colliding into her with fluid wildness, their clothes like the kindling on their explosion. Celina gripped his shoulders once more, dimly justifying the action as an attempt for balance, until her senses cried bullshit on her logic. The feel of his delts and traps, flexing as they gripped her, stole her breath as much as his erection at her core.

She was so mesmerized with exploring him, she didn't feel one of his hands move to the zipper of her skirt and tug it down. Only when his long fingers dived underneath, around the curve of her buttock, did she cry out in stunned awareness.

"Oh! Ohhhh..."

"Fuck." His hand spread, digging into her flesh, imprinting her skin with dark fire. "You feel so good..." He adjusted her weight so he could get his other hand in. "If you want me to stop, say something now, *stellina*. Otherwise..."

He'd paused as if to consider the finish of it, and that was a moment too long. Celina grabbed his head again and slammed his mouth down to hers in a new crash of passion. "Shut up," she finally told him, twining her breath to his with it. She heard his teeth lock from it and watched his eyes go a deeper shade of black, thick ink.

"Are *you* ordering *me*, Lieutenant?"

Though his challenge was dark as his stare, she still expected a little uptick of his formidable mouth. When it didn't come, she realized he was pretty damn serious about this. And, she realized with a jolt of amazement, she wanted him to be. The shock wave resonated through every cell of her body, most deeply in the secret layers now taunted by his fingers from the back and by his hard, pulsing pressure from the front. It felt like a tiny taste of what this could be, this vanquishing he hinted at, a battle and surrender and victory all in one night. It was clear the man went after his one-night stands with as much fervor as his company mergers. And tonight, if only for a few hours, she yearned to be desired that much. She wanted to be earned. She longed to be won.

That didn't mean she'd make it too easy.

"Perhaps I am, Mr. Tieri." She gave him the reply with a defiant jerk of her chin. "I'm comfortable with orders. Are you?"

His jaw worked back and forth a little. "That's a nice piece of lip, sweetheart, considering your back's to the wall with my hands up your skirt."

"Your hands aren't *up* my skirt."

"Well. Maybe your skirt"—he set her down so he could shove the cloth down, hooking her panties along with it—"needs to leave this conversation."

She gasped as the cool night air hit her exposed skin... and the moisture of her intimate folds. "Okay, that was an interesting order."

"It wasn't an order." He didn't give her time to generate a comeback, tugging her free from the clothes puddle and then slamming an urgent kiss to her again. "*This* is. Walk to your bedroom. Take the rest of your clothes off as you do."

The command turned her senses into another spirograph. The blatant carnality of it, along with the new steel in his tone, made her confused and aroused—and stupid and bold. "And is my voice is supposed to leave this conversation too?"

For the first time since she'd met Dante, there was a flash of color in his gaze. Holy shit. The man had deep, dark, incredible violet eyes.

In the next second, she also realized that the appearance of those purple flecks didn't exactly equate a good thing.

That regal hue also stood for royally ticked off. He proved as much by hauling her over again, smashing her back against his chest. His breath was a heated invasion in her ear as he worked the buttons of her jacket free with vehement twists.

"Two minutes ago, I told you to speak up, *stellina*. You kissed me instead." He jerked her jacket off her shoulders and shunted it down her arms. One of his hands stayed down there, landing sharp smacks to each of her ass cheeks. "Now move!"

A million retorts rocketed to her lips. Yet she couldn't set any one of them free. Her mind careened, trying to process what had happened. Had he really just *spanked* her? No. Seriously, *no*. She didn't do lusty. She didn't do wanton. And she sure as hell didn't do spanking.

But every inch of her backside was still ablaze from the blows. Every speck of her skin was a bloom of delicious warmth. And God help her, every inch of her pussy had gotten even more soaked, crying out in need for more...oh God, more.

Ohhhh, crap. Dante Tieri had just spanked her and then told her to lead him to her bedroom. And she was obeying. Gladly. Hurriedly. Trying to get her shirt and bra off as she did.

She was in trouble.

A lot of damn trouble.

CHAPTER FIVE

You're so in trouble.

The refrain pounded at Dante at least a hundred times as he watched what his spankings did to her—but worse, as he endured what *that* did to *him*.

First, her face had exploded in astonishment. Well, no shit. That was the expected part. But her attitude after that... *Hell.* He still stared, half-stunned, as her gape mellowed to reveal dilated eyes and a mouth parted in abject arousal. Not that she let him look at all of it for long—because she turned and actually conceded to his order, hurrying down the hall with her hands fumbling at her shirt and her ass, bright pink and gorgeous, swaying at him.

The ass he'd just whacked without a sneeze of approval from her.

Shit.

Oh, yeah. Trouble. Him. Same boat.

"Shit!"

He emitted it under his breath, mixing it with his confusion and anger. All right, sure, he'd spanked women before—right after they'd begged him to and usually right before a few other "hits" of things became more important. He'd never used the dynamic as real discipline, especially on a woman who'd already been pawed by barbarians tonight. Especially on a woman like Celina Kouris, period. She was an officer of his country's military, for fuck's sake. Couldn't she pull out some regulations manual, cite his ass for even touching her, and have him tossed in a damn cell?

The woman didn't look like she was considering that at the moment.

"*Shit.*"

He repeated it in a whisper as she stopped long enough to wriggle out of her shirt. She glanced back at him and licked her lips uncertainly. He gave her a small growl of approval, barely holding back from touching her again, as she rounded the corner into a dark room at the end of the hall.

When he entered the room, his eyes took a second to adjust. But only a second.

Thanks to the moonlight streaming through the shutters, Celina was the first thing illuminated for him. And, after he saw her, the only thing he really cared about.

"Oh, *stellina.*"

Now she really did look like a star come to earth, her nude perfection bathed in silver beams, her hair cascading around her shoulders, her eyes huge and deep. He didn't move for a long moment, for he wasn't stupid enough to think he'd ever get the gift of this sight again. She was perfect. So goddamn perfect.

She was also back to being visibly nervous. And lippy.

"Are you just going to stand there all night?"

He pressed his lips together and crossed his arms. Her feisty forest-cat thing, despite her obvious anxiety, was a massive turn-on. Not that he was going to share that. Not that he didn't crave to tame that wild creature this very second.

"Are you in a hurry for more orders?"

She jabbed her head forward with incredulous eyes. "More? Okay, wait. We're in here now, so why—"

"What would you do if I gave you more?"

Her little gasp matched a similar sound from his psyche. What the hell? He was a pretty passionate lover, but this was a path he'd never traversed with a woman.

Yet with *this* woman, it felt so achingly right.

"I—I don't know." Celina averted her gaze. But she shifted her thighs, and her areolas went deep red and tight around her erect pink nipples. "Your orders...they make me feel—"

"I know how my orders make you feel."

Again, she looked like she was going to slap him for that. But again she sucked the reaction back and simply looked to him. Nearly as if depending on him.

"Come here, Celina."

His voice now seemed to belong to another man, though it was definitely his guttural baritone wrapped around the words. When she stood but inches from him, he delved a hand into her hair and tugged her head up. He heard the little stop in her breath and wondered what that had done to her breasts. With his other hand, he rubbed a testing thumb across her nipple. Through it all, Celina remained exquisitely still, communicating to him only through the tiny cries that vibrated up in her mouth.

"Do you want to touch me too, *stellina*?"

She gave a tiny dip of her head and a sweet, acquiescing utterance. Without a word, with his lips still brushing hers, he pulled her hands up to his chest. The sound of her aroused moan was an aria. The feel of her fingers threading through his springy chest hair...heaven. A harsh sound erupted from him, and he filled her mouth with it as they fused into another kiss, tangling hard with each other now—but not hard enough that her hands didn't scratch their way down over his abs, scrabbling at the buckle of his belt and then the button of his pants.

Dante groaned. Beneath the fabric at which she fumbled, his cock pounded like a tethered bronco. He broke the kiss to toss his head back as she slid the zipper down the rise of his torment and then—

"Next order," he said, grating it. He refastened a hand into her hair and loved it when she sighed in response. He pulled harder and said, "Kneel for me, *stellina*. Then take me—damn!"

She dropped to her knees and pulled his cock into her mouth with a sweet, deep moan.

"Celina! Fuck!"

His thighs trembled and his ass clenched as the velvet of her mouth surrounded his burning length. With his hand still at her scalp, he gave in to the temptation to guide her pace, shocked when she let out a tiny mewl of arousal in return and pumped more feverishly. He couldn't take his eyes off the sight of her doing this to him. Her lips, so rosy and full, stuffed with his shaft. Her fingers, slender and graceful, braced to his thighs. Beyond that, he got peeks of her incredible breasts and then the dark-caramel curls that led exactly where he longed to taste next.

He finally pulled her from him with a reluctant yank. She started to stand, but Dante whirled her around and pressed her to the bed, her stomach flat against the white spread, her feet still on the floor. Her graceful ass was perfectly positioned in front of him.

"My turn," he declared, running his palms over both sides of her delicious globes. He hunkered behind her on the floor and brought both hands up to her thighs. "So fucking gorgeous, *tesorino*. Now spread them for me. Spread your legs wide. Dig your toes into the carpet. You will *not* move unless I tell you to. Are we clear?"

"Uh...uh-huh."

His wildcat sounded more a kitten with that, making the blood pound harder in his cock. Holy God, what her obedience was doing to him...was doing *in* him. As she opened her legs for him, obeying his directive to the letter, something surged in his mind and all five senses, something he'd never experienced in all his years of sexual adventures. It was heady, powerful—and when he saw everything it did for Celina too, it became outright magical. What the fuck had he stumbled into? He had no guide map, no sounding post. He'd never tried any of this with a woman before. But Celina Kouris, in all her headstrong, goddess-level, don't-fuck-with-a-navy-girl glory, was definitely unlike any woman he'd ever gotten naked with before.

He wanted to give her the moon.

Starting right now.

With that determination, he lowered his head to the moist folds between her legs and tasted her pussy for the first time.

Merda. She was pure ambrosia. A tangy, amazing cocktail of her essence and her arousal, flowing to greet him as he lapped at her with the flat of his tongue and then nipped her with teasing bites. But he was on a mission. He knew the sweet nub of flesh he wanted to get to, and he sought it out with careful stabs, seeking until he found—

"Ohhhh!"

Target achieved.

"Mmmmm." He drawled it as he hit her clit again. But this time Celina jumped beneath him, letting out an adorable yelp of pleasure. Before he thought about what he was doing, Dante reached up and smacked the meat of her ass in retaliation.

"What the—" She jerked again. He gave the other side a

hard spank. "Damn it, Dante! Why—"

"What part of the instruction wasn't clear, *stellina*? You told me you understood. And I told *you* not to move without being told."

"Are you freaking kidding?" At the two spanks he gave in answer, she shrieked. "Oh God! Dante—please! Ohhhhh!" She keened with the last of it as he reattached his mouth to the moist lips of her cunt. He'd returned to his ministrations partly out of curiosity. Did the blows coax even more of her cream out to play?

Damn straight they did.

He closed his eyes, sucking at her with greedy abandon, loving how she shook with the torment of staying still for him now. Soon, her gasps came faster and her whole body trembled. Her sobs gained intensity. She pushed back into his mouth, utterly ignoring his swats now, perhaps even wanting them.

It was the moment he pulled away.

"Dante!"

He grunted in victory as he rose, flipped her over, and slid her higher onto the mattress. "Yes, *stellina mia*?"

She writhed and bucked like she needed him to exorcise a demon from her. "You're making me crazy!"

He followed her onto the bed, but not before pushing her thighs back and giving her glistening pussy one last swipe with his thumbs. When he climbed there, replacing his fingers with his cock, he grabbed her hands under both of his, slamming her arms to the mattress above her head.

"No more crazy than you make me." He said it against her mouth, and she parted her lips in readiness for his kiss, but he didn't give it to her. Instead he hovered there, watching her intently as he worked his erection back and forth along her labia and clit, savoring the desperate, pleading little sounds that burst from her, loving the pieces of control she gave up with each passing minute, giving herself over to his rule. Her thighs clenched and coiled against his. She tried to twist her wrists from his hold, but that enforced his resolve to keep her trapped. Now compressed by his chest, her nipples puckered tighter.

"Oh!" She nearly shrieked it this time. "Please!"

"Yes, *cara*." He praised her, pressing his forehead to hers. "Give it all to me. Let it all go."

She trembled, wrenching in his hold again. "I—I don't know how—"

"Let me have it, Celina. That's all you have to do."

"L-Let you have what?"

"The control." He had no idea where that answer came from, but it fit. It more than fit. It was the truth. What he wanted from her. What he needed. "Stop fighting. Let me have it. Let me have it all as I get inside you..."

Remarkably, her arms went slack in his hold. She looked at him with eyes as brilliant as emeralds and forced in a breath. "I...I'll try."

He smiled his way into giving her a deep kiss. "Good girl." Locking his stare to hers again, he murmured, "Do you have supplies nearby, *stellina*?" Hell, he hoped the answer was yes, while bracing himself for the opposite. He had a condom or two in his wallet, but that was in his jacket back out in the living room, and things between their bodies were officially at level red in the potential detonation department.

"Supplies?" Her frown of confusion burst into wide-eyed comprehension. "Oh! Shit! Uhhh..." She blushed furiously, looking so damn innocent, he pulsed against her pussy with a new surge of readiness. "Nightstand," she said. "I think. Maybe at the back."

He'd already found the package, thank fucking God. He tore it open, noticing how Celina watched him with the fascination of a child looking at a balloon artist. He smiled, wondering how many times she'd really had a man in here, fishing through her bedside drawer for a rubber. When he pulled out the latex and her curiosity suddenly skittered, hiding behind a dropped gaze, he had his answer. There'd been nobody here before him. At least not recently.

Good. That was *really* fucking good.

He gritted his teeth as he rolled on the sheath, especially when he beheld her eyes on him again. Her mouth fell open, the tip of her tongue peeked from her teeth, and her eyes went from that bright jewel green to the shade of dark nettles. His flesh pushed even more impatiently at the condom, his head already taking a dip in the puddle of his pre-come, with every moment of her open desire. Thank crap the navy hadn't picked the woman for a covert-ops position. She wore every thought and emotion across her face and was the most erotic thing he'd ever seen for it.

"Damn. I need to do this." He rushed it out, the words potent with the need that shook him. "I need to be inside you, Celina. Now!"

She nodded. At least he thought she did. He lost all awareness as he lined up his hardness to her softness and got sucked into the incinerator of her tight tunnel. For at least a dozen thrusts, a hurricane could've hit, and he wouldn't have noticed anything beyond the ecstasy hitting his body through the funnel of hers. She gripped him, milked him, destroyed him, renewed him. But she cast her spell with more than what she offered anatomically. It was how she gave it to him, leaping outside every comfort zone she had to succumb to him in this way, even letting him pin her wrists down again as he thrust into her with long, deep, primal strokes of pure, pounding possession.

"Oh!"

She broke into her litany of sighs and moans to let it out. He stared at her, worried he'd hurt her somehow, especially when her head jacked back against the pillows, her neck straining. Then she called out again. "Please. Again. Oh please, Dante!"

A king-of-the-hill grin spread his lips. It had damn good justification. His name, pouring from her lips like that, and his cock, clearly finding her G-spot. Her muscles, trembling with the sensations he'd brought to them. This whole moment, ungluing the goddess inside this stunning woman. It felt like something prewritten in the stars, if he believed in bullshit like that.

He dipped his head, claiming the column of her neck with a hungry kiss before telling her, "Lift your legs higher, *stellina*. Wrap them around me. I'm gonna do it again, I promise. And I'm gonna make it really good."

She complied while teething her lip in a bashful smile, torpedoing his mind just like she had at the party. Only now, his body was part of the annihilation too. He gladly let the whole thing burn, surrendering as fully to her as she had to him. All the power she'd given over, the trust she'd shown, was now his gift back to her in the bliss he rendered to her body. She writhed beneath him, open in every way, her face a portrait of pleasure, her skin aglow, her breaths coming faster and faster until, in one starburst of a moment, she seized and screamed.

"Oh, Dante! Ohhhh, hell!"

Her fiery tunnel convulsed and throbbed, gripping him with every explosion of her orgasm. Panting against her shoulder, Dante managed three words before the glory of his own release came, mind-robbing and white-hot.

"No, sweetheart. Heaven."

CHAPTER SIX

Celina woke up with a jolt.

Where the hell was she?

The room was still dark. But it was her room. Okay, she was at home. So why did she feel so...off?

The clock on the nightstand read 5:30 a.m. Well, that much was normal. Unfortunately, her brain was preprogrammed for the time, weekends or not.

Weekends. Right. It was Saturday. Again, normal so far. She dragged a hand through her hair as the events of her not-so-normal Friday night began to hit. The froufrou party downtown. Her escape to the Blue Sax and the huge mistake of that decision. Then Dante barging in when those knuckle draggers had her cornered. Then Dante taking her home. Here. Then Dante—

Oh God. Then Dante flipping her world upside down and her body inside out.

"Shit!"

She whispered it, not wanting to wake him up. After what he'd done with her—done *to* her, even a second time—the guy deserved a little sleep. Warmth suffused her all over again at remembering how he'd massaged her into slumber first, after he'd gently toweled her off. She craved so much more of it all and was so tempted to scoot back under the covers and up against that honed sienna body of his, but it was time to put the fantasy away. Best to let him get out of here without the awkward goodbye and the empty promise to call her sometime.

If she sneaked quietly enough, she'd be out of bed and out the door to the gym before he even—

He wasn't there.

She ran her hand across the other side of her bed as if maybe he'd pulled an *Invisible Man* on her. He was definitely gone. But the sheets were still a little warm. And damn, they still smelled like him. Patchouli and musk stirred with her touch, reminding her all too clearly what they smelled like on his skin, under her tongue. The man definitely knew what looked *and* smelled amazing on his body.

She sat up a little straighter and heard him now. He was talking to someone, though his tone was deliberately subdued, so she couldn't make out the words. She listened to the timbre that constantly ran beneath his baritone, trying not to think how nice it sounded in the house, a perfect match to her hardwood floors and iron accents on the craftsman furniture. She scooted back against the pillows, lulled by the comforting sound of it.

That lasted for all of thirty seconds. She bolted up again. What the hell was she thinking? *Comforted?* No. *Lulled?* Hell, no. Dante Tieri was still in her house, and that should only be inciting one reaction in her. Anxiety. A lot of it.

That decision got her up and moving. And okay, so she routed through her drawer for her best sweats, bra, and T-shirt. So what? If she was going to toss a CEO hunk out of her house, she needed to look halfway decent, right? The same thought justified why she brushed her hair until it shined and then scrubbed her teeth followed by a mouthwash chaser. She felt better about seeing him already. Correction: confronting him. *Time to leave, buddy. Now. It was nice, but the party's over.*

Hell.

He was still breathtaking.

He lolled in one of her easy chairs, pretty much taking over the thing. He'd put his black dress pants back on but without the belt. They slung low on his hips, exposing the twin lines of muscle that led her gaze inexorably to his crotch. Trying to look away was equally exasperating because the panels of his open shirt were an ideal frame for the lightly haired planes of his dark chest. His hair was a tousled mess, an inky, tempting tangle that had her fingers itching to dive in again.

It was official. The man was just as mesmerizing after sex as before.

He turned when she walked in, winking but not breaking his conversation. "Okay, let's hold off on pouring the foundation for the marketplace until we have the secondary geo surveys back. I know it'll set things back by a few days, but we're not gonna do this thing half-assed, Parker. Yeah, Mexico City isn't coastal; so what? You and I both know that the Laguna Salada fault has swapped more than a little spit with the San Andreas. If they've had a secret geologic love child happening there, we need to know about it. Otherwise, we'll be pulling concrete back up and—" He stopped and looked at his phone. "Parker, I'll get back to you in a few. Gotta take this other line."

Celina pretended to putter around in the kitchen, pouring a cup of the coffee he'd already made, though she didn't hide her curiosity at what yanked him away from a business call so urgent, it warranted a five a.m. call on a Saturday. She observed his face through her lashes and then wished she hadn't. His face went soft, tender, loving. An expression like that could only be caused by a woman.

She raised the cup to her lips and glared at him over the

rim. The bastard was taking a call from another lover before even leaving *her* house?

"*Mamma?*"

She burned her tongue because she forgot to swallow the coffee. *Mamma?*

"*Sì, mi è.* Of course it's not too early. *Tutto sta bene? Lei è giusto? Come Aldo è?* No, I'm not at home." He gave an amused chuckle. "How did you know that? *Donna astuta.*"

At that moment, something started beeping behind Celina's butt. She jumped and then looked behind her in shock. What the hell was that?

"*Mamma,* I have to interrupt you. I need to get this frittata out of the oven."

This time, she choked on the coffee. *Frittata?*

"Here; talk to Celina for a minute." He said that part into the phone as he approached her and then kissed her lightly. Celina didn't have a moment for half a glare, let alone a protest, before he pressed the phone to her ear and then rushed off to the oven. Not that the sirens in her head hadn't picked up the slack in the distress signal department.

"Hello? Hello?" said a musical little voice in the phone. "Dante? *Agori mou? Ragazzo impetuoso! Dove è corso via a?*"

"Errr...good morning, Mrs. Tieri." Her voice shook like she was going through oral exams all over again. The woman sounded like she could spit tacks through the phone. She tossed a glower at Dante, who kicked the oven shut as he pulled out a steaming egg dish that turned the rumble in her stomach into a roar.

Just like that, the bristles in *Mamma's* voice melted. "Well...hello," she replied, her thick accent making the words more gooey. "Ah, now who is *this*?"

"My name is...er...Celina. Lieutenant Celina Kouris, ma'am. I'm...uh..."

"Is my boy taking care of you right, Celina?"

She glanced at Dante. He was slicing the frittata with a knowing smirk on his face that clenched her sex and spiked her ire. He probably knew exactly what his mother was saying— because she'd said it to a thousand women before her. "He's been a good friend." She pressed hard on the last word, hating that it merely thickened the heat in his eyes.

"Celina. I am Italian, *sì*? And this is the twenty-first century. No need for coy here. If he is handing the phone to you at this hour, I string the story together, *piccolina*. I just checking he's behaving right. Sure, he sends *me* the flowers all the time. How do I know what *that* means for anyone else? Dante, he tells me nothing! You are the first person I speak to in his life except Mark Moore. A mama needs to know these things. I did not raise that boy to be *un cazzo*."

"*Cazzo?*" she repeated, fighting her immediate affection for the woman. "Well, whatever that is, I don't think—"

"Mother!" He lunged and grabbed the phone. "*Mamma,* you can't go throwing out words like—I know, but—*Mamma,* I tell you plenty. I know she's the first woman since Demi—" He darted a glance up at her and then commanded to his mom, "Can we get back to what you called me at five in the morning about? Is everything all right? Is Aldo treating *you* right? *Sì,* I know he's been your boyfriend for two years, but—" He listened for a moment and then chuckled. "Well, you assumed right. I usually do pick up best at this time. And you're welcome. I'm glad you like them. No, six dozen is not too much. Christmas roses are your favorite. *Mamma,* I need to go. *La chiamerò dopo. Ti amo. Ciao.*"

He clicked the phone off with a little shake of his head and then tossed it back to the couch. With that, his full attention now swung directly on her. He bent his head toward her, the midnight force of his stare pulling her closer. Celina scrutinized him harder. The deep-purple cast she'd seen in his eyes last night—there were only tiny flecks of it at the corners this morning.

Morning. Yes. She remembered now. It was morning. It was Saturday. It was time for him to go, before she let him reach out to her...as he did right now. Then twine his fingers into her hair, like he also did now...only way better than last night, since he now knew how sensitive she was along the top of her ear. And she certainly couldn't let him lean in and kiss her, exactly like he did now, taking his time with the torment, parting her lips to touch her tongue with his.

"Good morning, *stellina*," he murmured. "Are you hungry? I made a frittata."

"Uh, yeah. I see." Despite her sardonic tone, it took every ounce of will to untangle herself from his hold, pretending she needed more coffee. "I'm not too hungry yet. I'm not much of a breakfast person."

Her stomach outed her, revving like a lawn mower. Dante's lips quirked, making him even more flat-out gorgeous.

"Uh, yeah. I see." He used her own words in his comeback tease.

She eyed the heavenly frittata, made with eggs she barely remembered buying. And the other ingredients? Well, the cheese made sense. She always had cheese lying around. It was a weakness. But the rest of it confused her. All the colors mixed into the food—where had he found all that? Had he called Vince and had the guy schlep over groceries for him too? Or did the millionaires of the city share a secret twenty-four-hour produce delivery service? It felt surreal to even be contemplating those explanations. And overwhelming. And magical.

And good. Damn, he made her feel very, very good.

Right. Just like Mom had felt with Mr. Bank Bastard. And Natalie, with her commodities prince.

"I...errrm...don't use the kitchen much."

"You don't say."

She hardened her stare. "I usually don't have Cordon Bleu-trained billionaires in here either."

The barb hit home. Dante looked like a man now about to slip his boxing gloves on. "Is that so? So who *do* you have in here?"

She folded her arms, feeling oddly naked in front of him again. "My brothers, sometimes. But most of the time, just Sami."

"Sami." The remainder of his grin drained. His posture stiffened. "Really?" The casual tone was riddled with barbs. "And who's he? And how often is he here?"

"He?" For a second, she was confused. Then she was tempted, just a little, to string out *his* misconception. But subterfuge was as foreign to her as fried crickets. "Well, *she's* usually here a few times a week." She tapped Sami's spring school portrait, stuck to the refrigerator with her favorite USN magnet. "Samantha Karena Kouris," she explained. "Sami for short. She's my niece."

His smile returned, only twice as blinding as before. "Ohhhh." Relief was an obvious wash on his face. "Well, she's beautiful."

She touched Sami's picture lovingly. "She is, isn't she? I

love that kid. We're working on her science fair project this weekend. She's redesigning jet fighter engines to restart in midair."

He chuckled. "Is that all?"

She couldn't help but return a smile. "Nothing like a little ambition. But with a dad who flies those planes, there's no mystery to her intent."

"Your brother?" Dante asked. She nodded before he ventured quietly, "Why isn't Sami's mother helping her with the project?"

Tension returned to her stomach. She didn't know why. This was a good bridge into walking him politely out the door. "Sami's mom isn't around. Apparently a billionaire in a private jet was more appealing than her soldier in a F-16 Viper."

Dante scrubbed a hand across his beard and then winced. She didn't know whether to interpret his action as pissed or stunned. Maybe both. "Shit," he muttered.

"Oh, yeah. A nice pile of it. I tried to warn Dylan before he put the ring on her finger. There was something *off* about Natalie. She wasn't real. She gazed at clouds too much. She was too much like..."

"Who?" He spoke it into her weighted pause, his voice as gentle as the day's early light, now peeking through the shutters.

Celina swallowed past the rock in her throat and forced the answer out. "Like Mom."

She could practically hear the gears sliding against each other in Dante's brain. "Okay, wait. Your mother ran off with a Trump wannabe too?"

The words, even infused with his amazement, hit her heart like punches. Again, she ordered herself to respond.

"I was nine. He was the president of the bank she worked at. Guess she just couldn't deal with three hellcat boys and a girl who wanted to be like them." A dry laugh escaped her. "My poor brothers. I can't cook worth crap. They lived on boxed mac and cheese for years."

"Damn." It was a harsh bite of sound. Oddly, that comforted her. His ire on her behalf—it was sweet. Actually, more than sweet. And sweet on the inside, mixed with his just over six feet of hard-core sexy on the outside, was doing things to her inner resolve that weren't comfortable.

She took a deep breath. She needed to keep this in perspective. She needed to keep *him* in perspective. Okay, she'd slept with him. And maybe a little more too. That didn't mean anything had changed. She wasn't ready to go inviting him back over for Sunday dinner or sharing more with him besides the coffee. If anything, maybe he would see that now too.

Finally, Dante spoke again. "That certainly paints the picture more clearly."

"The picture?"

"Of you. Of why you treated me like a criminal last night. Before you even met me, you had me signed, sealed, and delivered as a hump-happy barracuda."

"I didn't treat you like—"

She huffed and then went silent. What was she supposed to say? That he was wrong? That he hadn't hit the nail on the head about everything? That she didn't stand here and stress, every second, that she was going to be just like Mom and Natalie—especially because she wanted him more as each of those moments ticked by? That having him so near, eating up the air in the kitchen with his dark, bold perfection, didn't wind temptation around every nerve center in her body? God, if only his shirt were buttoned. And his fingers, so long and strong, were stuck in gloves. And maybe if there was a paper bag over his face, which halted her breath even now with its accusing glower...

"Look, it was a nice time." She attempted a nonchalant shrug and a flippant smile. "You're not a criminal anymore, okay? So...we're good?"

She dared to glance up. Big mistake. His jaw worked back and forth. The violet flecks in his eyes were now a wash of fury. "Nice. Huh. Thanks for that. Glad to know you enjoyed yourself."

"All right, fine. It was better than nice. But—"

"But now it's time for the barracuda to swim away, right?" He pushed up from the kitchen bar, looking ready to tear the thing out instead.

"Dante—"

He lunged next to her again in two steps. The suddenness of the move literally made her head swim. Damn it, she could actually feel his body heat. "Look at me, Celina. *Now.* Look at me and tell me again that last night was just 'nice.' Or do you always let men pull you out of bar fights and then take you home and spank you before they—"

"Stop it." She shoved at him. "That's dirty tactics, Tieri!"

"That's *truth,* Lieutenant Kouris." He wasn't just ticked anymore. He was relentless. She had to back up as he kept pacing but finally had nowhere to go when her back bumped the pantry. Dante spread himself around her, surrounding her with his size and scent and strength, locking her gaze into his without a shred of mercy. "You wanna know what I think?" His voice was low and lethal yet prowling and knowing. "I think last night was fucking amazing—for both of us." He lifted a hand to brush her cheek with his thumb. "I think you're a revelation to me, Celina. And I think I may be one to you as well."

"Dante." Her pleading rasp was horrific to hear. "Please. Don't."

"When was the last time you got to let go? The last time you gave yourself permission to?"

He'd gone beyond slamming nails on the head. Now he was a damn wrecking ball, gouging into her with scary precision. And he was everywhere. His thighs, huge and hard. His chest, rippled and warm. And his gaze, shot with merciless, beautiful tanzanite. She needed to get free. She couldn't let herself drown in him again.

"Stop it."

"No." It wasn't a response. It was an order. "Tell me. *Tell me,* Celina. You liked handing it over to me, didn't you? The permission. The control. You have to keep it together all the time, don't you? Never any room for error. You're the good lawyer. The good sister. The good aunt. The good friend. Deviance isn't an option. Orgasms sure as hell aren't an option. At least not with someone like me. Someone who'd dare to command you to come—"

"That's enough!"

Tears broke up her words, but concrete infused her arms. She shoved at him so hard, he stumbled back against the sink. She twisted away, bracing her hands against the cupboards. The panels had glass panes in them, showing off her china, now taunting her with its stark-white perfection. Crap. Even her damn dinner plates confirmed what Dante had just said. Her world had no room for deviation. But because of that, it also had no color.

No deep-bronze skin. No raging violet gazes. No dark-crimson lips, fusing her mouth and opening her senses...

No complications. No pain. No heartbreak.

It was better this way. She just had to keep telling herself that. She'd find a way to breathe normally again. She'd find a way to *think* normally again. Probably. Hopefully.

"Maybe I should just go."

His flat murmur made her fingers twist into fists. She heard him push toward her because of it. Panic set in. She tensed. He stopped.

She couldn't let him get near again. Not ever again.

"Y-Yeah," she stammered. "Yeah, that's—that's a good idea."

"Celina—"

"Please go, Dante. Please."

As soon as he scooped his cell and his jacket up and then quietly shut the door, she heard a car engine start. For a second, curiosity took over her sadness. Did the man have time to buy himself new wheels *and* have them delivered while making her a frittata and handling business deals?

A peek out the front window answered that. A gorgeous black Jag sedan idled out in front while Dante climbed into the front passenger's seat. There was another man in the car, with a chiseled face, a military-grade buzz, and a no-nonsense way about him. She pegged him as the oh-so-reliable Vincent.

As soon as Dante buckled in, the car sped away.

She resisted the urge to sprint after it.

Ha. Like that would be possible, considering how every muscle now dragged her like a lead weight, making the whole house echo with the emptiness of her steps.

"Stop it."

The words she'd used on Dante two minutes ago were now her self-castigation. She called up her resolve by punching both arms down and then marching to the kitchen and picking up the pan with the frittata. With a harsh sigh, she flipped on the disposal motor and scraped the beautiful mess down into the grinding maw.

Thank God garbage disposals worked on tears too.

★ ★ ★

After the fifteen-minute meltdown, she didn't think about Dante again all weekend.

Okay, maybe that one wasn't going to slip past a polygraph. But it wasn't like she didn't try. And most of the time, her efforts yielded success. It was only when the unexpected moments sneaked up on her: those tiny torpedoes that barreled her over and pummeled her through the waves of longing once again. Hearing him get thanked on the B96 morning show on her way to the gym. Changing the sheets on the bed and having to smell him everywhere on the air. And, worst of all, facing Dylan when he brought Sami over before his duty rotation and weathering her big brother's wide smirk. "Well," he'd drawled. "Somebody's glowing today. Did my little baklava actually bring home somebody fun from the V-Day party?"

Though he stood nearly a foot taller, she'd drilled him hard enough in the shoulder to make him wince. Sami squealed and cheered her on, clearly wanting blood, reminding Celina way too much of herself at that age. But she couldn't find it in her heart to chastise her niece, grateful as hell to have the bouncy kid around for the rest of the day and a sleepover to boot. Sami's presence, even with nocturnal thrashings, was better than the alternative: the empty pillows next to her. The memories of Dante's dark hair spread against them. The feel of his body around her and his breath against her shoulder...

Remembrances that waited until Sunday night to torture her instead. All night.

Which was why, as midmorning break rolled around on Monday, she joined Eve and Reiley by way of a stop at the coffee cart for a large latte with a double shot.

"Whoa." Eve tucked a stray red curl behind an ear as she eyed the tall cup. "Fueling up a little early today, Kouris?"

"Rough night," she mumbled. "And this custody case is sucking it out of me too."

Rei frowned in sympathy. "Still Lieutenant Braden?"

Celina sipped her drink and nodded. "His wife can't see past her own selfish ass about this. Just because she's got some cushy gig and a fancy new CEO boyfriend in Tokyo now doesn't give her the right to sue for full custody. Zell is a good man. He was special ops, he did shit he can't even tell me about, but he gave it all up, asked to be reassigned here as a trainer at RTC so Zach could have a stable upbringing. He's been there nearly every day for that kid. And Cassandra took that as *her* open invitation to gallivant across the globe with a shitload of playboys. I hear she's about to sign some new reality-show deal too!"

Reiley patted her hand. "Careful there, cowgirl. Your personal agenda is showing juuust a wee bit."

Eve chuffed. "I'm more impressed that she used 'gallivant' in a complete sentence before noon."

Celina's phone saved her from composing a decent comeback to her friend. She looked in the window to check the caller first but rose as she did, expecting it to be the return call she expected from Zell Braden.

She froze. Her coffee slid so hard from her other hand that it splashed a little on the table.

In the window, she read: *Global Restoration Incorporated.*

There was only one person she knew at GRI. He'd left her house on Saturday morning, fuming like a pit bull—and sucking the atmosphere from the whole place with him.

She clicked Ignore. Then sat back down, unable to hide how her legs shook with the effort.

Eve's brows lowered. "Okay. You want to tell us who *that* was?"

"No."

"No?" Reiley echoed. "Seriously? The color just drained from your gorgeous Greek skin, honey."

"Nobody important."

Dante didn't let her get away with that. The next second, her phone turned into a Mexican jumping bean with a string of texts.

We need to talk.

Friday was significant. I know you felt it too.

Celina, CALL ME.

Dinner. I'm only asking for dinner.

Do you want me to keep this up all day? I'm clearing my schedule now.

"Damn it!" she muttered. He was persistent as a pit bull

too, which meant that eventually he'd get tired of his new "play toy" and move along to something new, probably in the neighborhood of a 36-C chest, a mass of mermaid curls, and hefty stilt heels to hold it all up. But before that happened, she refused to let him toss her around in his frenzy. It was torture. It was heaven.

It was one night that would never go any further.

The phone vibrated twice more before she could delete the other messages. Her teeth jammed together. "How the hell did he even get this number?"

"He?" Eve perked up like a three-year-old tempted with a candy bar. "Whoa. He who?" Before Celina could react, her friend snatched away the phone. "What're you holding back from us?"

"Eve! Shit!"

Eve's jaw dropped. "*Shit* is right. Friday was significant? What the hell? Friday...when? Nothing happened Friday, except at—"

"The party!" Rei finished it off with a voice spiked in excitement.

"But you left," Eve stated. "You went to the Blue Sax." She stared in accusation. "You texted and said you'd caught a cab home."

"Yeah." She fumed. "And that's exactly what I did. Give me my phone back, Eve. I'm not kidding."

"But you weren't alone, were you?" Her friend looked at the screen again, and her eyes widened. "You went home with somebody! And whoever it was had a pretty great time too."

"C'mon, Eve. Please."

"Wow," Reiley interjected. "This feels big. It was either completely shitty or pure heaven."

Eve placed the phone back onto the table. The move was

slow and solemn. "Okay. Whatever. We're just your two best friends. If you don't feel the need to share, then—"

She was interrupted when another call started vibrating the phone. The thing still lay faceup on the table, now visible to all three of them. Celina prayed that this time it was Zell Braden.

Again, the screen flashed *Global Restoration Incorporated*.

Eye and Reiley gasped in unison.

"Oh my God." Reiley's whisper sounded like they stood in the Sistine Chapel. "Right after midnight, Dante Tieri disappeared from the party."

"Yeah," Eve concurred. "And fast." She looked up at Celina with her wide green gaze. "And you were the reason why...weren't you?"

Reiley let out another rasp. "Holy crap, Cel. You slept with Dante Tieri?"

Eve snorted. "I'll bet there wasn't a lot of sleeping going on."

"And now he wants to see you again! Shit! Cel!"

Celina grabbed her phone and rose, failing at making both actions seem anywhere near calm. "It's not happening. *He's* not happening. And no, I'm not going to 'share' about it." She felt her friends' hurt curl through the air like acrid smoke. She felt shitty about that, but it didn't change her determination to push Friday night into the past. The *far* past. "Things sometimes happen, okay? Anomalies are only that. Nothing more."

"Anomalies?" Eve tossed a disbelieving glance at Rei. "She did *not* just call Dante Tieri an *anomaly*, did she?"

Celina rolled her eyes. "Fine. You want a better word? How about mistakes? Yeah, that *is* better. Mistakes happen, you guys. That doesn't mean one needs to repeat them."

Before either of them could hold her hostage again, she grabbed her coffee and then left the lounge without a backward look. That didn't stop Eve from lobbing a parting shot, directed at Reiley but deliberately loud enough for her to hear too.

"I wish *my* mistakes made me blush like that."

CHAPTER SEVEN

Dante ordered a fourth Glenlivet on the rocks while finishing off his third. He set the empty glass on the bar and studied the leftover condensation on it, collecting the blue-gray lighting off the back bar. Delilah's was a perfect pick for tonight, his and Mark's go-to choice for enjoying whiskey, pool, and conversation without worrying about the social page editor taking dictation on their words. Not that he gave his friend much to go on so far. That didn't stop Mark from sharpening up the scalpels in his gaze or hunkering his leather-jacket-covered shoulders in a lame attempt at unobtrusive.

"No reserve chute tonight, eh, Inferno Boy?" Mark finally drawled.

He cocked his head at his friend. The liquor finally started to work, creating a warm fuzz in his head. Well, wasn't that nice? It did shit for the chill he couldn't get out of his blood, the emptiness since he'd left Celina's on Saturday. The void he didn't even know he'd been living with until the party *this* guy talked him into throwing.

"You called this meeting, boss, not me."

The bartender brought him his new drink, but as he reached for it, Mark clamped a hand on his arm.

"All right, Tieri. Start talking before you're not able to."

Dante took a quaff of the whiskey out of pure defiance. Mark huffed.

"Is it the company? Something with the family? Is your

mother sick?"

"No," Dante snapped. Hell, the man would just keep ramming if he didn't. "No, no, and no." He dragged a hand through his hair. The room felt too small. His skin felt too tight. "Fuck. If only it were that easy."

He should've expected his friend's reaction. A knowing snicker leaked from Mark's lips. "Okay, got it now."

He glared again. "Really? All figured out, huh?"

"Shut up, Tieri, and tell me who she is."

Dante brooded into his drink. He'd let the guy crow about getting that far into his head. But the rest? *He* couldn't figure out the rest. And damn it, he liked being miserable about it. The gloom gave him a reason to think about her. To hang on to her somehow.

"All right, then. I'll assume it's Suzanne Collins. Personally, I didn't get the connection with you two on Friday, but—"

"Shut up." He practically snarled it. "Are you kidding me? Suzanne? Don't you know me better than that?"

Mark cocked a brow in arrogance and swigged his beer. "Guess not. But I'm all about enlightenment."

Damn it. Now the fucker had him backed into the proverbial corner. No wonder Marker Man was in demand to consult with every major company in the city, not to mention the senate wanting him back. He scowled again at his friend's serene profile and then muttered, "You remember the JAG officers...the three who approached us at the party?"

"Ohhh yeah." A grin breached Mark's lips. "The two little ones were cute. Didn't they stick around for a while? But of course, you fixated on that leggy brunette. The one who glared like you were every box in her 'no' column checked off. Man, she did not like y—" The guy broke into a knowing chuckle as

Dante's face tightened. "Hell. It *is* the brunette. You dog! How on earth—"

"Long story. Too long. Let's just say I ended up escorting her home. Let's just say things progressed from there. Fast."

"Okay. So what's the problem? Was it shitty sex?"

"No." He polished off the whiskey and flagged the barkeep for another. "No. *Fuck.* No. It was..." He grabbed a napkin and twisted the thing until it shredded. "Let's just say I'm surprised the roof stayed on, you know?"

Mark glanced in confusion. "For her as well as you?"

He closed his eyes for a second. All too clearly, his mind filled with the beauty of Celina's face against the pillows, the ecstasy of her body around him. His cock pulsed in his jeans, still craving the feeling of her vagina squeezing him as he'd brought her to orgasm. She'd come even harder the second time, when he'd ordered her to grip the headboard while he slammed into her from behind and thumbed her clit with every thrust.

"Yeah," he finally said. "She—uh—well, it was mutual. Yes."

He watched his friend barely contain a smirk. "Usually that's not a problem, Dante."

His new drink arrived. He was shocked he didn't shatter the glass as he gripped it. "Usually I don't do what I did on Friday, either."

"Oh?"

He squeezed his eyes shut again. When he opened them, the room started to swim a little. Thank God. The whiskey simmered in his blood none too soon, bringing with it the words he'd never be able to utter sober.

"Celina's different, Mark. She's smart and strong...and

lippy and defiant. She brought out shit in me..." He gave his throat another handshake with the Glenlivet. "Fuck. I had no idea where it came from. Jesus, I—"

A fast glance at Mark didn't turn up a shred of judgment on the man's face. But there wasn't understanding there either. Hell. He was going to have to say it.

"I struck her, man. I did it hard. And not just once."

Three seconds of assessing silence bounced back from his friend. Then Mark said in a calm undertone, "You mean you spanked her."

Dante swallowed heavily. And damn it, fought to forget the other body parts getting heavy as well. His balls felt like chunks of coal, and his cock was a battering ram, just from the memory of how his hand had felt on the firm globes of her ass. "Yeah. I—I guess you could say that."

"And you liked it."

He stared at his friend. "How can you be so conversational about this?"

"Just answer the question. Did you like it?"

"Yes, goddamn it. I liked it, okay?" The room tilted in commiseration. Who was he kidding? He'd loved it. He wanted more of it. *Now.* More of taming her fire, harnessing her lightning, making her scream and writhe and orgasm for him.

"Fuck!" He couldn't keep the memories from filling his mind.

"And you probably liked the rest of it too."

That shaved a discomfiting hunk off his buzz. "What the hell do you mean, the rest of it?" he snapped. "There *was* no 'rest of it'!"

Mark frowned. "No pulling her hair? No growling a few

orders? Having her get into position and stay there?" The man's mouth ticked up. "No loving how that made her turn to putty in your arms? And maybe a few other consistencies too?"

"Shit."

"So there *was* a bit of the rest."

He clawed his hair again. "I'm at least ten years older than her."

"Doesn't fly in my book, Tieri. Look at the woman who put this bastard's ring on her finger." He thumbed his chest.

"Yeah, but you didn't throw Rose over the bed and whack her ass to—" He stopped when he focused enough on Mark's face to see the affirmative glints in his eyes and the growing grin beneath his gold beard. "Holy shit." Both words came out as growls. "Hell. We're a couple of goddamn perverts."

"No, my friend. We're a couple of Doms."

He raised a brow. "What?"

"Doms, Dante. *Dominants.* People who enjoy being in control. Men who like nothing better than taking the lead during a sexual sequence and controlling every second of a woman's pleasure. And for many of us, when that woman makes us earn the privilege of her submission, the experience is even more...errmm...addicting."

Dante dug a hand into his hair again. He stopped when his palm hit his forehead. "Addicting," he echoed. "Jesus. That's a good way of putting it." And a lousy way too. He needed another hit of Celina Kouris and highly doubted there was a detox program for shit like this.

"I'm just a little stunned you didn't know this about yourself until now."

"And how long have *you* been doing this shit then, spanky?"

Mark shrugged. "I was about twenty-two when I discovered the lifestyle. I was just damn lucky Heather liked it too. Of course, the Dom/sub world wasn't what it is today. Clubs were still in people's basements. There wasn't as much education about things, and—"

"Wait. Back the truck up. Clubs? There are *clubs* for this stuff?"

Mark chuckled. "Yes, my friend. With my public profile, Rose and I can't exactly keep a spanking bench and a St. Andrew's cross in the corner of the bedroom. We're fond of a few private places in town known for their discretion and private rooms."

Dante let that sink in while he ordered a glass of water. Sobering up fast became a priority. He was exhilarated and perplexed at the same time. So much of the way he was wired now made sense. He was Italian, for Christ's sake; sex had been part of his vernacular since he was a kid. But until Friday with Celina, it had also been a simple physical act he could leave behind as easily as a used condom. Now, he couldn't stop thinking about what they'd done and how they'd done it. With this new chunk of knowledge, he felt like Columbus in the New World. Terrified to stay. Terrified to leave.

"And Rose goes to these places with you?" he queried. "Willingly? Knowing what she's going to let you do to her?"

"What I'm going to do *with* her, yes. She's my collared submissive as well as my wife."

"Collared..." Recognition flared. "You mean that little choker she wears around the house—"

"Signifies that she's committed to me as a sexual submissive. It also represents my commitment to her, as her Dom, that I'll never abuse the gift of her surrender and I'll always make sure she gets what she needs from our dynamic."

"When you go these clubs."

"Most of the time, yes."

Dante couldn't help slashing an incisive stare at his friend. "And she's fine with all this?"

"Kid in a candy store is more like it." Mark chuffed and chucked a wadded cocktail napkin at him. "Don't snort, asshole. I'm serious. Last month, she even surprised me for my birthday by securing an overnight suite at Dark Escape. It's become her favorite club, I think. She likes the eucalyptus in the aftercare lotions."

"Aftercare." Dante leaned close again. "That sounds key. Explain."

Mark paused, seeming to read him. Definitely knowing, as his best friend, that he didn't bother to pick apart something with a hundred questions unless the subject was important. Really fucking important.

"All right, let me ask you this. What did you do for Celina when you were—er—finished with things on Friday night?"

"Cleaned her up. Gave her a massage." He stopped just short of saying *the usual,* though that would've been the truth. As for after that? All right, those parts weren't so usual. "All right, so I spent the night. Then I kind of made her breakfast."

Mark nodded and gave a big grin. "Breakfast. Not bad."

He shrugged. "Just a frittata."

His friend's eyebrows jumped. "A *frittata*?" He tossed his head back, laughing. "Inferno, just check this one off. You'll have no trouble picking up on aftercare."

The remark, meant as encouragement, wreaked an opposite effect. As the water flushed everything from Dante's skull except a headache, another aftereffect of sobriety barged in.

Rationality.

What the hell made him think he'd be "checking" anything off Mark's magical checklist anytime soon? Okay, he was a Dominant. It was a missing link for him. A huge one. It also explained why he couldn't let go of the woman who'd helped him discover it—and brought him no closer to doing so than before.

Which made him wish he'd stayed shit faced.

"No," he muttered. "I don't think I'll be *aftercaring* anything or anyone soon, man."

He expected the line to be the stumper for his friend. Instead, Mark nodded knowingly again. "Aha. Now we're at the meat of things." He tilted his head back. "Let me see if I can get this right. Your Celina got up and didn't even look at your frittata. She looked at *you* like you suddenly had a pumpkin for a head, got you out the door as fast as possible, and then hasn't returned the hundred phone calls and three hundred texts you've left her since. And you think if you keep pounding at that door hard enough, it'll cave, and she'll be standing behind it, ready to change her mind. Am I close?"

Dante didn't answer. He hailed the bartender and ordered another drink. A double this time.

"I'm that right on the money, huh?"

"It doesn't change a thing, you fucker."

Mark didn't volley back to that. Dante assumed the bastard would finally let him return to a drunken stupor in peace, until the man turned on his bar stool and fully faced him.

"You want to know why I've got this so right? Because I went through the same thing with Rose. Okay, I didn't cook her a goddamn frittata; you superachievers really piss me off sometimes. But the reaction? The terror in her eyes? The whole look that says 'what the hell did I just let this man do to me, and why did I love it so much?' Been there, man. Done that."

He inhaled hard against the lead weight in his chest and returned his friend's direct stare. "So what did you do to change her mind?"

"Kidnapped her."

He waited for the I'm-just-shitting-you grin. It didn't come.

"What do you mean?"

Mark shrugged and gave a lopsided grin. "All right, so I did let her walk onto the yacht under her own choice. But after that, she was mine." He blinked only once. "I tied her up. Made her listen. Forced her to feel and experience the beauty of her submission, to accept that surrendering to me unlocked something in herself she couldn't ignore."

"The yacht," Dante repeated. "So this was when you two were still at the training in the Bahamas?" When Mark nodded, he whistled low. "You don't waste time, Marker Man."

"Remarkable women don't come along every day." He leaned over and clapped Dante's shoulder. "Let me guarantee you one thing. If you two really blew the roof off her place, then she's still confused too. She still can't stop thinking about it either—and you'll never have a better opportunity to fight for her." His brows kicked up a little. "*If* you want to fight for her?"

He returned his friend's scrutiny so hard, his jaw ached from clenching. "What the fuck do you suggest I do? Kidnap a US Navy JAG officer, carry her off on a goddamn yacht, and tie her up until she listens?"

"In a manner of speaking, yes."

"Excuse me?"

"Methods should be modified for the subbie, my friend. I think your friend Celina might react to a more literal approach. And I believe I have just the secret weapon to help us achieve that."

"What exactly is that?"

"Not what." He pulled his cell out of his pocket and punched a button. "*Who.*" His smile deepened. "Hello, my pet. How are you? No, I'm still here with Inferno Boy. I'll be home soon. I called to ask you a question. How would you like a field trip to Dark Escape?" He held the phone back a few inches as a high-pitched shriek erupted through the ear hole. "I think that means she's in."

CHAPTER EIGHT

Celina glanced at Eve and Reiley again as they hurried from the "L" station and crossed Jackson Boulevard, hunching their shoulders against the knife of icy wind cutting up from the river. The street banners flapped over their heads, making it look like the cartoon turkey on them had invented a new dance step. She wondered if the big guy would be boogying in some snow during his big parade this year.

She stopped and hesitated as they got to the doors with the gleaming letters declaring they'd arrived at the Willis Tower. The two of them must have spiked her coffee yesterday morning, because she still couldn't believe she was here, tagging along for yet another party. "Because last week ended up so well," she finished in a dark mutter.

"What are you grumbling about back there, Kouris?" Eve called above the beat of her platform party heels as she led the way into the building.

"Pascal, are you absolutely sure this is where Trev's party is?"

She knew Trevin Nash was turning thirty. She also knew he'd do anything to make an impression on Eve. But a birthday bash at the most iconic skyscraper in the city, still called the Sears Tower by many because it was that famous, seemed out of budget even for their cocky coworker.

"Cel, just go with the flow for once, all right? This is gonna be...fun!"

Something felt weird about the pause in her friend's statement. Eve was genetically wired to spit out the word "fun" every fifteen minutes or so. But her voice had definitely hitched, even if her sashay hadn't. Celina shot a look of concern at her friend's leather-jacketed back. Maybe she was starting to have cold feet about Lieutenant Nash and all his swagger. That was just fine by her. Just because the guy worked for the navy didn't mean he wasn't as flash hungry as a private-sector attorney. But bling was an irresistible siren to Eve too. On the other hand, Eve hadn't watched what money could do to people. How it broke hearts and lives.

Great. Hadn't she picked out the perfect mindset to bring into a building like this? Celina clomped along behind her friends in a pair of black high-heeled boots Reiley had persuaded her to buy on sale in June. Their footsteps bounced off the lobby's gleaming floors and shiny walls, making the place sound like a basketball court, if basketballs were now made of million-dollar bills. She tugged at her skirt, now wishing she hadn't also let Rei talk her into wearing fishnet hose with her outfit.

"Would you stop that?" Eve chastised as they got onto the elevator. "Your skirt's so long, people can only see two inches of the hose anyhow. And I can't believe you wore a turtleneck too."

She glowered at them both. "I feel totally out of place. Like Julia Roberts at that polo match in *Pretty Woman.*"

Reiley glared. "You look like Julie Andrews, circa *The Sound of Music.*"

"Before she left the convent," Eve added.

"Way before," Reiley asserted.

The elevator got to their floor. Celina didn't even pay

attention how high they'd come in the building, but if her mild vertigo was an altitude barometer too, she guessed they were well past halfway. She got off the elevator after her friends and entered a lobby that dripped of opulence, elegance, and a classic Hollywood vibe of romance. Indigo and red velvet drapes were complemented by matching settees and understated lighting. The black carpet was so thick, it felt like treading on memory foam. Music played through hidden speakers, a throbbing dance beat turned soothing by strings and a singer who mixed Madonna's eroticism with Adele's soul.

Not the kind of music she'd expected to hear at Trev's birthday bash.

Not the kind of place she expected Trev to pick at all, actually.

"This is weird," she murmured. "You guys, don't you think this is weird? Is anyone even here? Are we sure this is the... right..."

She stammered into silence as a figure seemed to materialize from the curtains. A black T-shirt outlined every hard striation of his tapered torso. Charcoal cargo pants covered the endless inches of his legs. Leather biker boots encased his feet. His ink-dark hair was a rough tumble against his set jaw. And then she confronted that deep-as-midnight gaze, shaded with just a hint of indigo, enduring its probe straight into her psyche, trembling as it stabbed right into her sex.

And fuming as Dante lifted a slow smile.

He knew. He just knew, didn't he? He could see her thoughts, knowing that every moment of Friday night flooded back to her in a dizzy rush.

She stumbled backward and grabbed for the curtains.

Like that helped. The room turned into a fun house anyway, tilting wildly on her. She tottered again, feeling as ridiculous as a clown in that fun house. Guess that was what fury and exhilaration did when they hit like taunting squirt gun blasts.

Her mortification doubled when he closed the gap between them in three strides. "Easy, *cara*." He braced her arms like she weighed no more than a feather. "You okay?"

"Easy." She threw it back from tight teeth. "Easy? You're daring to use that word on me right now? Really?" She squirmed, but he didn't let go. She swung out a glare at both her friends. "Don't *either* of you even think about some half-baked apology right now!"

"Who says we're sorry?" Eve countered.

A giggle—a giggle!—spilled from Reiley, who hadn't even left the elevator. She adopted a coy pose, holding the button to keep the doors open. "I'm just sorry we're the ones who have to go."

Celina ripped a stare between both of them. "Ohhh no! Wait a second! You guys aren't—"

"They'll be right up the street, *stellina*."

Eve nodded. "Trev's party is actually at Muldoon's. It's right around the corner. We're a phone call away. Honest."

Celina huffed. "*Honest* isn't working so well for you right now."

"And *denial* hasn't been working great for you this whole week, Cel." Damn it, the little redhead pulled out her I'm-right-and-you-know-it stance. "He wouldn't have had to resort to this if you'd just returned a phone call."

"Thank you," Dante murmured.

"Shut up," Celina snapped.

"Damn it, Cel." Her friend added a glower to the pose.

78

"Why don't you give him a chance?"

Celina dropped her head. She refused to let them all see the conflict that was certainly twisting its way across her face. *Because I gave him a chance already. In a moment of hormones, pheromones, and crazy, I gave him way more than a chance. And I liked it. No, I loved it. And I can't love it again. I can't let him in again. I'm not a key acquisition for Dante Tieri's relationship portfolio!*

He dissolved the diatribe with his next words, given in a low, sincere tone. "One hour." He slid his grip down to her hands. "Celina. *Cara*. Sixty minutes is all this will take. After that"—he nodded toward Eve and Reiley—"you'll call your friends, if you want to."

"What do you mean, *if* I want to?" She snapped another glare as Eve stepped back to the elevator. "Would you two stop laughing?"

Reiley tossed her hair over one shoulder and waved with her fingertips. "Mr. Tieri? If she turns down the request, I'm available."

Eve high-fived her for that, but Dante acknowledged it with only half a smile. The focus of his gaze and the pressure of his grip never veered from Celina. Both intensified as he stated, "It's not a request."

★ ★ ★

What the hell was this place?

She'd wondered it at least twelve times as Dante guided her, one hand at her back, out of the lobby and down an equally plush hallway. The lighting on the corridor had been even more evocative than the entry, broken only by little spotlights that illuminated graphic prints on the wall. Each picture depicted a pair of hands joined together—simple, right?—only the photographer had captured a passion in the clasps that was captivating, arousing.

Terrifying.

She struggled to shove the word out of her head as they entered a small sitting room populated with a soft black leather couch, a huge matching easy chair, and a kitchenette area. There was another door on the opposite wall, next to the chair. No hands tangling on the walls here. The large print hanging over the couch went straight for a close-up of locked thighs. One set was smooth, the other muscled and rough. And the positioning made her think of—

Things she couldn't be thinking of in a room alone with him.

"Your sixty minutes is now fifty." She lowered to the couch, purposely getting the wall print behind her.

Dante went for the big chair. Without a break in his movement, he pulled her across and then down into his lap. "Fifty-six, actually." He showed her the timer on his watch. "I'm a man of my word, *stellina mia.*"

She winced. "You need to stop calling me that."

"Why? *My little star.* It fits."

"Really? And how many other women have you made it 'fit'?"

Though that strange smile hadn't left his lips, his gaze gained a velvet thickness. "Only you."

She drew breath to push out a scoff. He silenced it with two fingers on her lips.

"When I first saw you, I thought you looked like a goddess from one of my grandfather's mythology books." His fingers drifted across her cheek, trailing soft heat across her skin. "Then when I learned your name...*Celina*..." He gave it an Italian twist that was entirely too sexy, accenting the first syllable like *cheh*. "Well, it's perfect. She was one of the daughters of Atlas, you know. She was transformed into a star of the Pleiades by Zeus."

"Uh-huh." Celina murmured it gently but managed to get her brows into mocking arches. "Right after they killed themselves."

"Okay, there was that." He moved his touch from her cheek to the skin in front of her ear. "Proving the axiom that death can, in rare instances, be a turn for the good."

She spit out a laugh. What alternative had he given her? "Dear God. And I thought Greek men were morbid!"

"Death is just a transformation, Celina. Change. And change is often good for you." He delved his hand to her nape now, tightening his fingers to her scalp, a physical command for her full attention. "Sometimes very good."

Breathing. It was supposed to be involuntary, right? Then why did she have to cue her lungs to the act as he pulled her even closer, making her take in the glittering heat in his gaze and the determined set of his Roman lips? *Do it. Take in air. Stay alive so you don't die like this, in the arms of a billionaire player who doesn't really care about you, who only wants the conquest of you.*

"Y-You kidnapped me to tell me this?"

He didn't blink. As he spoke again, his lips barely moved. "What we shared on Friday night changed *me*, Celina. And I'll bet you've been thinking about a few new things too."

She closed her eyes. It was her only recourse against the consuming nearness of him. His arms were so steady, so sure.

His breath had a hint of brandy to it. She wondered if his lips tasted just as delicious...

"Dante, please. It—Friday—was nice. But—"

"Nice." He deepened the touch at her waist. "What part of it was nice?"

She swallowed. Like that helped. "You seriously want a debrief?"

"Stop evading." Both his grips twisted hard now, and her pulse doubled. "Answer me." He shifted, nearly becoming a dark shell around her. "Have you ever let a man do that to you before? Put his hand on your ass and spank it into that beautiful shade of red?"

She sighed as his breath fanned her neck, as her mind slipped deeper into the tunnel of his presence, his power. She couldn't do this. She shouldn't be here. He was everything she didn't need, everything that screamed *wrong*.

But everything that felt so right.

"N-No." It spilled out in a whisper. "You were the first."

When he smiled like she'd given him a precious gift, her body flooded with warmth. She longed for him to kiss her, but he looked like he had more to say. A lot more.

"I've never done that before either."

She blinked past the flash bomb of shock. "Excuse me? You're kidding, right?"

He let out a heavy sigh. "We'll get into your strange preconceptions of me later. For now, you need to roll with that as the truth." He dipped his head toward her again, turning his body into a cavern of sheer possession. "I liked spanking you, Celina. I liked it a lot. And I know you liked it too."

She felt him leaning her back a little more, easing her neck against the chair's wide arm. The erotic print on the wall teased from her peripheral. "Y-Yes," she admitted. "I liked it."

"I couldn't stop thinking about it." He started trailing soft caresses between her hip and rib cage. "And I thought I was going out of my mind at first. I thought I'd become some kind of abusive freak. But remembering how you reacted to me, how you came alive with it—it felt significant for both of us. Then I'd swing back the other way, assuming you couldn't possibly be on that same seesaw...and terrified of what you likely *were* thinking instead."

She had to remind herself to breathe again. "You were really scared?"

"You mean the stalker calls and texts didn't clue you in?" His touch became a gentle massage at the side of her breast. His stare gained a hundred more fathoms of dark-indigo intensity. "Fortunately, a friend caught me before I resorted to camping on your doorstep. He set me straight about a number of things, actually. Turns out I'm not a freak after all." He dipped even closer, nearly grazing her lips with his. "I'm a Dominant."

The way he spoke that last word, like wanting to try it on *her* for size, zapped Celina's nervous system with a swarm of impulses. Run. Stay. Slap him. Hold him. Get out of the rabbit hole. Now.

"Congratulations," she muttered. "S-So what does that make me?"

"That's what we're here to find out."

"Excuse me?" Her new version of the phrase came spiked with a little amazement and a lot of alarm. She lifted her head, taking in the surroundings with fresh understanding. The lighting. The music. The artwork. Most of all, the focused purpose he hadn't let up on since she got here.

I'm a Dominant.

It wasn't like she'd never heard the word before, even as a noun. She had three brothers, for freak's sake. Three big, horny, slightly more than passionate brothers. She'd gotten good at translating their "guy code" over the years. So she knew "Dominant" and even "submissive." But those words—and places like this that went along with them—belonged in the world of Dylan, Nik, and Cameron, not her. Not to the point that she'd sleep with said Dominant again. Not to the point that she'd willingly stand in a room with him a second longer.

"No way." She shoved from him and bolted to her feet. "No, Dante. This isn't going to happen, okay?"

He rose with the grace of a damn devil lord from one of her teenage romance novels. Just as smoothly, he glanced at his watch. "You still owe me forty-two minutes."

"So we're going to use the time constructively, is that it? I'll bet that door leads to a nice little kink den where you've got rope and a row of paddles waiting. You got me here to 'illuminate' me about my submissiveness, right?"

The devil lord exterior hid the reflexes of a fox. Within seconds, he regained the space between them and coiled a python grip around her arm. "At this point, I wish I really could take you *anywhere* and paddle you. Would you open your mind for one damn minute?" He hauled her close, nearly against his chest. "I've been through a little bit more of life than you, Celina. Maybe that doesn't take precedence in a bunch of the tidy little categories in your code book of the world, but it does here." He grabbed her other arm. "What we have, what we've found in each other, it doesn't fall off the universe's tree every day, *cara*. And yes, that scared the shit out of me at first. I thought I'd taken this connection to you, something I hadn't had with a woman in so damn long, and then severed it by unleashing some strange, horrific animal."

He wasn't joking. Not a bit. The realization pulled her hands up to his chest. "You're not an animal. Well, not a horrific one."

"But you reacted the same way too." He gently lifted her chin. "Didn't you?"

Celina wet her lips. "It doesn't matter, okay? It happened, and now it's over—"

"And you're lying." He thumbed away the two tears that seeped and betrayed her. Oh, hell. This was such a bad idea. She'd practically seen the quiver of emotional arrows he carried from the second he'd appeared in the lobby, each of them dipped in the vat of memories from Friday, acting like acid on the bricks of her willpower. "It still matters to you as much as it matters to me. And you want to know that you're not a freak either." He dipped his face and kissed the rest of the moistness off her cheek. "You're not, *stellina*. Not ever with me." He took her lips too, brushing them in a sweet caress. "What you gave me on Friday, stripping off your goddess, giving yourself to me as the pure woman you are... It was beautiful. Amazing."

She felt her walls starting to dissolve beneath the onslaught of his seduction. A ragged sigh spilled from her. "Thank you," she whispered. "Thank you..."

She tipped her face up, craving for him to kiss her more deeply, but he left her drowning in that desire, pulling back with an intent set to his jaw. "Come." He tugged on both her hands, leading her toward the room's second door. "There's something in here that we both need to see, to discover. Together."

Celina resisted. "Dante, I don't think—"

"I don't want you to think." He stopped, turned, and lifted

one hand to her sternum. "Not right now. I'm not asking for anything from you in here than your openness. To observe. To absorb. To feel with all the reaches of your heart. I'm asking for your courage, *stellina,* and your trust. Can you commit those to me just for forty-two more minutes?"

She dragged in a hard breath. Another. She was certain he could feel her trepidation, pounding like a Chippewa tribe on the warpath, right through her skin. But she was also certain, as their stares met and locked, that he saw the answer brimming on her lips. The word she'd been so determined not to give him. Damn it, the rabbit hole was already rising up and sucking her down to an end that would collapse like a house of cards and a voice—her own—screaming "off with her head!"

Still, she swayed toward him. She looked at every perfect demon-god line of his face, fixed on her with a potency she'd never experienced before, pulling her like every beautiful Lucifer that Dylan had warned her about when she'd hit puberty. She'd been so good about resisting "those" kind of men, until now. Until a hurricane named Dante Tieri hit to her senses. Dylan had never prepared her for someone like him.

And she had no will left to fight.

"Yes." She gave it to him in a clear, sure voice. "All right. You're right. I owe you at least forty-two minutes."

"*Us,*" he clarified. "You owe it to us, Celina."

She showed him her opinion of that with a massive eye roll.

Then let him turn and open the door—into a room that made her stare do anything but roll.

Holy shit. What had she gotten herself into?

CHAPTER NINE

Dante had seen the playroom when he first got here, when Mark gave him a tour of the club—but the sight of the space now, with the lights lowered and the equipment in place, put it into a new perspective even for him. The black walls had subtle lighting aimed at them in flesh-colored tones. The only other light came from a few pin spotlights in the ceiling, gelled in red and purple. Those lights were aimed at several pieces of furniture: a double-level bench, a large-frame truss lined with hooks, and a leather swing hanging from another truss that resembled the skeleton for a tepee. Mounted along one wall was a large black steel rack, which had been empty during the tour but now displayed an array of long paddles, leather floggers, and other implements of sensual promise. Dante concluded those must be the contents of the bag Mark had brought with him and dropped in front of the rack during the tour.

As he expected, Celina took two steps in—and then gasped and froze.

As he also expected, everything between his hips ignited. His cock was the burning branch that led the way.

He had to ignore both those factors right now. *Fuck.*

Celina wrenched her hands from him and whirled for the door. He was ready for that too and snatched her back by one wrist.

She practically hissed back like a soaked cat. "Damn it, I

said this wasn't happening!"

He kept his reply regulated. "And I didn't argue. I'm a man of my word, *stellina*."

She rocked back on one foot. "Really now?"

"None of this is for you."

He watched her reaction carefully. Though she covered it fast, there was a flash of surprise and then disappointment. That masquerade took so much effort, she forgot to avert the open stare she gave everything in the room...more than once. Dante took a deep breath to keep his own features schooled and his hard-on in check. The first was simple, the second sheer hell. Okay, she was curious. That was encouraging but a long way from wanting to rush in and try everything. He still had to be prepared for what she might do at the evening's next turn of events.

Like his thought had summoned the event, the door on the far side of the playroom opened. Mark filled the doorway and then entered on a confident stride. He was dressed identical to Dante from the waist down, though his torso was encased differently. He wore a simple gray fitted tank, and black leather gauntlets encased his muscled arms from wrist to elbow. His gaze glittered like the gold of King Tut's tomb, and an equally pagan grin parted his gold beard.

In short, he dripped with the essence of an entirely different person than the guy Dante usually knew as his best friend.

"Shit." His stunned mutter was due to more than just the wardrobe change, even more than the "Master Mark" who'd unveiled himself during their conversation at Delilah's on Thursday. Dante still couldn't believe where *that* casual meeting had gone. He'd learned more about his friend in one hour than he had in the previous three years. Amazing, eye-opening stuff that had helped him learn and accept a huge part of himself in the process. He'd heard about Mark's own discovery of his Dominant side, followed by the blessing of meeting and marrying Heather. He'd also watched his friend get out the difficult truth of how it had felt after she'd died, how he hadn't even tried seeking a new submissive, for he'd basically concluded such a miracle was impossible. Then he'd watched new life burst onto Mark's face when he began talking about Rose.

The words Mark had given him then were what made him finally agree to this crazy plan tonight.

"Dante, my friend, when the gods smile upon a Dom with the gift of a subbie with a spirit, a will, a heart, and an ass that fit perfectly with him, then that Dom is an idiot not to fight for her. Fully. Fervently. Ferociously."

So here he was, still shaking in his boots—literally—though he made a good pretense of relaxed as he moved to greet his friend, giving him the once-over again. "Well." He chuckled. "What a difference an hour and some leather can do to a guy."

Mark spread his arms, showing off the gauntlets. "They were a birthday gift from Rose. She gets all gooey when she sees me in them." He smirked. "So needless to say, I wear them to bed every night."

Dante chuffed. "Marker Man, I think you'd do just fine without them."

Mark's attention switched to Celina. Though his smile warmed, not a shred of his commanding demeanor lessened. "Good evening, sweet girl." His gaze swept her from head to toe. "That navy uniform didn't do you justice. She's stunning, Dante. No wonder you're here fighting for her."

He grinned in gratitude. Mark always came through with the words to make *him* shine. "Damn straight," he affirmed, pulling her close. A little more hope spiked when he felt no resistance in the press of her body.

"And, ummm, what exactly is *here*?" she asked then.

"Welcome to Dark Escape," Mark replied. "Let's say it's a clubhouse...for special kinds of fun and exploration. Don't worry, Celina. It's very private, members only. Your identity is safe. *You're* safe. It's the first point of what we're here to help you explore tonight. It's also the most important."

That was when she pressed a hand to Dante's ribs and tried to push away. "Look, I—I'm not some repressed submissive, waiting to discover my sexual freedom and—"

"Funny," Mark replied. "That's nearly word for word what my sweet pet said before she let me unleash her." He gave a cocky wink. "Of course, she looks so pretty *on* a leash too."

Celina gasped.

Dante glared. "Not helping, man!"

"Sorry. It slipped. Honestly, Inferno."

He ignored his friend's little smirk, yanking Celina close again. This time he stepped in front of her, bracing her face and making her look up at him. "What have I asked you for, *stellina*? I haven't taken more than a kiss from you tonight. My purpose is to *give* you something. Understanding. Awareness. To know that what we tasted Friday night wasn't something weird or wrong—that it was beautiful, right, and rare. Mark and Rose have agreed to help us see more of that." He brushed her temples with his thumbs, relieved to see tiny glimmers of interest in her gaze. Reluctantly, he dropped one hand to curl it against hers. "You can handle thirty minutes of enlightenment, can't you?"

Though conflict still skittered across her face, she finally gave him a jerky nod. "All right."

Her fingers trembled against his, and he lifted them to his lips. Without another word, he led her to the large leather chair tucked in the corner, a twin to the one they'd just shared back in the anteroom. Like before, he sat and then pulled her into his lap. But unlike then, her limbs were now stiff logs in his hold. She didn't spare him a glance. Tension wrapped her. Again, this was either really great or really shitty for his cause. He glanced at his watch. He now had twenty-nine minutes to figure out which one.

CHAPTER TEN

Shit, shit, shit.

If her heartbeat wasn't pummeling her chest to the point that it hurt, Celina would've written this off as a dream. An insane, bizarre, *why the hell did I just dream all that?* kind of thing. A secret bondage club? Hidden in the Willis Tower? With Mark Moore and his wife as members? And her, sitting here about to watch them, with Dante Tieri's lap as her voyeur post?

She took it back. This *was* a dream. Which meant she was about to wake up and wouldn't have to process any more of what was going on. She wouldn't have to deal with how much faster her pulse kept speeding or how that beat of hot blood made itself most known in the folds between her legs, where she was discernibly, uncomfortably soaked now.

A dream. A dream. Wake up! Wake up!

But her breath came faster as Dante eased her deeper against his chest. His own heartbeat felt magnificent beneath her ear, especially when the playroom door opened again and Rose Moore came into the room.

Mark Moore was a stunning man, but he became radiant when turning and seeing his wife, who wore her mahogany hair long and loose and was dressed in a stunning black shift. Celina was riveted by his face. She didn't think she'd ever seen a look of such deep devotion before. But her fascination turned to total absorption when she watched how Rose looked back at him. The woman went from sublime to glowing in the five seconds it took her to reach her husband. Her dark eyes turned to rivers of deep emotion. She closed them in bliss as Mark grabbed her hair at the scalp, pulled her head back, and plunged his tongue into her mouth. Celina swallowed hard as the kiss went from possessive to carnal. She wondered how Rose summoned the self-control to keep her hands at her sides as her husband kissed her longer, harder. She watched as Rose's hands curled on themselves, fighting the urge to touch him. Even that was strangely moving, especially when Mark used his other hand to bracket her cheek, stroking her there with steady, certain command.

The moment felt so raw and intimate, Celina forced herself to look away. But she didn't find much relief in the doing. Her face ended up inches from Dante's. How long had he been watching her? More importantly, how long had those new dark-amethyst glints been in his gaze, like he craved to kiss her in the exact same way? She knew it took about three seconds for *her* mind to be consumed with the thought. And the tissues of her sex to flood with the hot, beating need.

Mark's growl actually came as a welcome attention grabber. Celina looked up to find he'd released his wife from their kiss with the sound. As soon as he did, Rose dropped her head and then the rest of her body. Celina watched in fascination as Rose slid to her knees before her husband, her hands dropping to the tops of her thighs, her body a beautiful line of perfect posture. In return, Mark's hand never left her hair. He rotated his hand in deep, sensual movements, almost as if massaging her, letting out an even more primitive sound as she leaned into his thigh, sighing in pleasure.

Celina didn't want to love what she watched. A woman

sinking to her knees for a man, from just a kiss? Then practically snuggling his crotch like a kitten, coaxed only by his touch? Forget about shoving the woman's movement back by a hundred years. This spun the gender role clock back to the Stone Age.

But maybe that's what felt so right about it.

She watched more closely as Rose lifted her face and smiled at Mark. His stare was completely wrapped in her too. They looked at each other like they were the only man and woman in the world. Their bond was formed with a language that needed no words, entwined with an energy that was part of their DNA. A man and his mate. A leader and his helper. Primal and simple yet more complex and perfect than every damn psychology book out there.

Celina slanted her head as another revelation struck her. At Friday's party on the dance floor, Rose Moore had been the embodiment of the modern sass-and-fire wife. But at the feet of her man, she was a woman come full circle in herself. She hadn't given up any part of herself to do this. She'd added to all of it—with a magnificence that made Celina smile.

"You please me, pet," Mark murmured then. He stroked the top of her head.

"Thank you, Master," she replied.

"You remember your safe word, honey?"

"Yes, Master. It's *worth*."

"Perfect. You also remember we have visitors tonight, yes? Are you going to help me show them more ways you can be good?"

She leaned her cheek into the palm he pressed against it. "Oh yes." An eager smile parted her lips. "Yes, I want to please you and them."

"Mmmm...yes, honey. So up with you now. On your feet, love." He helped Rose stand again but released her right after she had her balance, and then he leaned against one leg of the large truss. "Take off the dress for me, pet. Look at me as you do."

Celina took a shaking breath. With the grace of a dancer, Rose peeled her shift over her head. By tantalizing inches, her creamy skin and a red leather bustier with matching panties were exposed. The woman had the figure of a curvy Hollywood pinup idol, and that was clearly fine with her husband.

"Damn." Mark's gaze went visibly dusky, even from across the room. "The red leather. Oh, pet, you know how I love the red leather."

Rose nodded but didn't move otherwise. She must have given Mark a taunting look, because he broke into a hearty chuckle. "You're really proud of yourself, aren't you? Daring minx. For that naughty tease, you'll lose the corset first." He stepped around her, backhanding a swat to her tush as he started toward the rack of handheld implements against the wall. "Off. Now."

She tossed a pout at his back. "But I just put it on."

Celina grabbed Dante's hand before she could stop herself. Her knowledge of all this was a line drawing at best, but even she already saw that Mark Moore meant business tonight. She rested a little easier as she caught the smile Rose inserted at the end of her rebellion. Maybe the woman knew damn well what scary buttons she was pushing in her very authoritative husband.

But maybe not.

In a flash, Mark whirled back and caught Rose by the arm. "I know damn well when you put it on, pet." All the gentle edges of his voice were gone. Low precision took their place. "But after you stepped through that door, who did it belong to?"

Rose's answer came on a rough rasp. "You, Master."

"And who says when it comes off?"

"You, Master."

"And who did you turn your safety, your body, and your spirit to when you came in here?"

"They all belong to you, Master."

A guttural hum of approval accompanied his slide of fingers up over her bare shoulder, making Rose's breasts pump against the corset with her rising heartbeat. She tilted her head, offering her neck to him, clearly begging for more. While Celina's pulse surged the same direction, she again felt her head warring with her heart. To need a man's contact that badly—it couldn't be right.

Yet as Dante slid a hand up to her nape, gripping her with the same hard possession, she'd never craved anything more. Or felt more right in letting out a word of breathless entreaty. "Yes..."

Dante didn't say anything. Neither did Mark. The Dom pivoted away from Rose, leaving her gasping and swaying as he went back to the rack on the wall. Rose quickly got to work on taking off her corset. It laced in the back but had hooks in the front, which she detached with urgent twists. Her breasts came free, the centers already tight and dark around nipples that were high and erect. She bit her bottom lip as she pulled the corset away. As a woman newly pregnant, just the kiss of the air was likely as stimulating as hell to her.

She was beautiful.

The fabric against Celina's own skin suddenly felt like a

straitjacket. It was a thought she should've pulled back as soon as she had it. She'd forgotten how Dante had that damn mental X-ray and how he'd made a very good career of exploiting the talent.

In one smooth shift, he changed their positions in the chair. Suddenly, she was no longer in his lap. He pressed her forward over one of the wide arms, with the wall of his torso encasing her from behind. As her body acknowledged his nearness, her head tumbled further down the rabbit hole.

Just as he slipped a hand beneath her top and unsnapped her bra clasp.

"Yes!"

She was unable to control the exclamation but felt awful about it. She and Dante were sexual spies, leeching on something special between this couple. But then Rose and Mark smiled her way together, almost like approval, as if her outburst were applause. Though they were across the room from each other, she felt clasped to Rose now, bound to her by a strange yet awesome sisterhood. Rose's smile grew as if she recognized the connection too.

Sisters.

She'd never had a sister.

She shook her head, fighting that Lifetime movie stupidity. Why the hell was she reading so much into this? This was only about great sex. Wild, intense, off-the-charts sex, for certain, but—

"My my, pet." Mark's lust-heavy declaration was her perfect diversion. It looked that way for Rose too. The woman dipped her head as her Dom approached, though she sneaked peeks at Mark through the fringe of her dark lashes. She watched him latch a pair of suspension wrist cuffs into bolts along the top of the truss, her breasts shaking a little with her breaths, though she went utterly still as he swung to brace himself in front of her again. As he ran his gaze down her body in open appraisal, he murmured, "Much, much better."

"Thank you, Master. I always want to please you."

"And you do." He lifted both hands to her breasts, stroking the coral nipples with his knuckles. "Damn, Rose...that child is already being good to these lovely tits."

Rose's face contorted in arousal. Her breaths turned into small sobs as Mark bent his head to softly kiss her abdomen. Hesitantly at first and then encouraged by her man's moan, Rose lifted her hands and tangled them in his hair.

Mark groaned again, though deeper. He trailed his mouth up her body in a variation of nips and suckles that made Rose grip him tighter, mewling and whimpering. "Please, Master."

His mouth slid along her collarbone. "What do you need, pet?"

"*More.*"

When he got to her mouth, he gave her just that.

The lovers crashed together, sweeping and devouring each other. Mark hauled her nearly naked form against his big body. Rose fisted one hand in his hair, the other in his shirt. As she watched them, Celina couldn't move. Her whole body shuddered, surging in awakening as it too confirmed what she was watching. Power exchange. Give and take. Mark took his pet's obedience and rewarded her for it by lifting her to him, with him, completing him. They weren't just Dominant and submissive, nor even man and woman. They were simply one.

She'd never seen anything more beautiful.

Nor had she felt anything more magical when Dante's fingers slid across her erect nipples.

She clenched her jaw to keep a scream from erupting as his harsh breath fanned her ear. He pinched her harder as Mark and Rose kissed like taking their last taste of each other. She pushed her chest more urgently into his touch, needing more herself, craving the tiny jolts of pain. When he squeezed tighter, she gasped. A river of arousal started in the deepest tunnel of her body.

Dante maintained the pressure as Mark spun Rose around and jerked her arms over her head. With deft movements, he quickly had his wife latched into the suspension cuffs.

"Comfy, honey?" He gave her the query on a deep drawl.

"Yes." Rose's stretched body was a breathtaking portrait of creamy curves. "Yes, Master, thank you."

"You'll show me your thanks in a minute or so, pet. Right *here*." He gave her ass another solid spank, just before pulling out a pair of scissors from a pocket and slicing the leather thong at one hip. She let out what sounded like a sigh. Mark stopped, arching a brow. "Is there another problem, honey?"

"No, Master." Her voice was edged with resignation. "You did, after all, buy me six pairs of those."

"Damn right." He repocketed the scissors and stood behind her, jerking the leather down the rest of the way and letting it puddle at her right ankle. "Because I'll be waiting right here, ready to cut them and watch them slide off this beautiful ass again."

While he spoke that, he scraped his fingers across her backside. Another growl rumbled out of him as the skin went pink beneath his assault. Rose answered him this time with a soft moan. Celina heard her teeth grinding together with the tension of keeping her own breath in.

"Don't." Dante's voice vibrated in her ear as his hands

fanned her rib cage. "Don't hold it back, darling. Hearing your pleasure increases hers."

She wanted to tell him to shut up. She sure as *hell* didn't want to become sexual modeling clay in his hands again, especially like this, in this place that felt even less like reality than her bedroom on Friday night. She was deep in the abyss now, unable to grab any ledges of logic. And the fall was glorious. She was consumed by the beauty of what she witnessed, longing for more of the sweet cadence in her pussy and the music in her blood.

Dante wouldn't let her get any further into her head. He nudged the hair from her ear and then bit on it. "Let. It. Out." His command was a whispered snarl.

As Mark Moore landed a loud spank to his wife's ass, Celina obeyed.

Her broken cry mixed with Rose's high keen.

Seconds later, Rose's scream turned into a long and low groan. Her hips started circling. Her head lolled to the side. She snapped it back up as Mark delivered two more smacks and then repeated the treatment. Celina lost count of how many there were in all, but when he finally came to a pause, Rose sobbed in a mix of pain and ecstasy, her body trembling, her knuckles white against the support rungs of the cuffs. Her ass was a bright bloom that matched her name. Mark ran his hands across those dark-pink planes in possessive adoration.

"Fuck, honey. This is the most beautiful thing I've ever seen. You're so hot for me right now, aren't you?"

As if to prove it to them both, he slipped a hand down and pushed several fingers into her core.

"Yes!" Rose shoved her hips at him. "Yes, Master. Thank you..."

In their corner, Celina couldn't restrain herself from doing the same thing. Her body moved as if another willed it, thrusting back into Dante, seeking deeper contact. He responded with a coarse grunt of approval, his breath scorching her neck.

Mark shifted to Rose's side, though he still pumped his hand into the cleft between Rose's thighs. His other hand now bracketed her jaw, leading her gaze toward his. "What do you need now, pet? What can your Master give you? You need to speak it." He leaned and licked the seam of her slightly parted lips. "You need to beg me for it."

Rose shuddered like just his command was a gift. "Don't stop," she pleaded. She raised her face higher, pushing her lips toward his, totally aglow in the attention he focused on her. "Please, Master...I need more."

Celina's lungs pumped. Still, she couldn't seem to get air. She didn't care. She couldn't rip her eyes from the raw beauty of what she beheld. The open, sweet gift of this submissive. The powerful but tender guidance of her Dom. The promise of fulfillment, sexual and emotional and spiritual, that they gave more deeply to each other with each passing second. She wasn't just transfixed by the sight. She was elevated.

Something sawed into her mental tree house. It was a persistent buzz, vibrating against her shoulder until Dante stopped it. His cell phone? No, it was his watch. Why was his Tag Heuer making like a disgusting fly right *now*?

He spoke into her ear again, though now his voice wasn't sensual. It was laced with sadness.

"That's the alarm, *stellina*. Your hour is up. You're free to go."

CHAPTER ELEVEN

Dante had never been more thrilled to see a woman glare at him.

He had no idea where he got the strength to pull away from her, much less rise to his feet. Or how he extended his hand to help her up. Or kept from grinning like an idiot when she glowered at his fingers. And he *really* didn't know how he maintained that control as conflict took over her features.

He endured a second of sharp guilt. He'd forced this struggle on her and now watched it twist across her beautiful features. Did she leave now and forget all this, denying everything that was clearly awakened in her because of it? Did she just go to her friend's party, shoving aside how this experience, as sudden and startling as it was, made her see what they could be together? Or did she stay and consort with the enemy? Could she admit the enemy might not be the enemy, that maybe *he* was the universe's "gotcha" on all that armor around her soul?

Her stare climbed from his hand to his face. He strongly wished he'd had the sense to borrow some of her armor. Her emerald eyes were large, luminous, and lost. He swallowed and locked his body in place. He couldn't take away her agony. Not this time. He wouldn't force this decision on her. He'd asked for an hour and gotten it. The rest was up to her.

She took a shuddering breath. Another. For a moment, Dante forgot other people were in the room. He forgot air was in the room.

She reached up a trembling hand and twined it into his. "Can I stay?"

The words were barely breaths, but they blasted cannon holes into his composure. He rode the explosion, not waiting for Celina to pull him back down. He yanked her up to him, slamming her full against him and waiting for her with the hungry crush of his kiss. Fuck. *Fuck.* She was more soft, fragrant, passionate, and perfect than he remembered. Her mouth was a deeper, more delicious cave. Her hips were a more ideal fit against his. Her ass filled his palms as if made for them, a revelation he took full advantage of, kneading her sweet backside. God, she felt amazing.

She felt right.

Across the room, a sharp rhythm cracked the air. Rose's high gasps synched to it. From the sound of it, Mark had graduated from manual spankings to sensation play of a more creative form. Earlier, Mark told Dante he was likely to honor this special occasion by pulling out Rose's favorite forms of discipline, which meant the woman's ass was now getting reacquainted with their crop or their padded paddle. That wasn't the part that turned Dante on. But Celina's reaction to it—*merda*, she was obliterating him in chunks with it. Her throaty sigh was hard enough to bear. Her fierce grip into his hair, even harder. But when she started stabbing her tongue against his in time to Mark's whacks, he was pulverized. The only standing pillar in his body was the one between his thighs, screaming at him in need and engraving his zipper on its throbbing length.

No. No, damn it. He and Mark had talked about this part as well. The part about wanting to flatten one's woman to the floor—or the bed, the wall, the table, the chair—and spread her wide for ultimate annihilation. This part, Mark had told him, occurred regularly and had to be trained for behavior just like a good flogging hand.

He tore his lips away, punctuating with a determined growl. Celina's stare threatened to engulf him again, a thousand frightened questions swirling in the dark-green depths. Her desire was there too, an entrancing sheen. She was so breathtaking, ready, and open. Her bravery stunned him. Moved him. And holy hell, did it arouse him.

He had to get those eyes off him.

With another grunt, he spun her around. He tugged both hands into the bottom of her turtleneck. "Off," he ordered into her ear. "Now."

Celina helped him pull the sweater free. Her hair tumbled down, a sweep of lush sable against her smooth olive skin. The sight stoked his sexual furnace even more when the bra he'd unclasped also fell free. Now she was bare from the waist up, like a gorgeous servant girl offered for his pleasure. And, judging from the tight nipples that met his touch, *her* desire too.

That fantasy thickened as he and Celina refocused on Mark and Rose. Sure enough, Mrs. Moore was fully attending the needs of her Master, who paced behind her trembling form as he stroked the tongue of a leather riding crop along her upper thighs. The woman's ass wasn't a delicate bridal blush anymore. It bloomed a hot red. There were even a few burgundy marks scattered along her skin. Rose looked far from hating the treatment, however. The woman's head rolled to the side, her eyes closed in ecstasy, her lips panting in excitement.

Celina let out a gasp. Dante wondered if the reaction

stemmed from mortification or arousal. She didn't make him wait long for the answer. As Mark began another series of crop strokes on his wife, Celina's nipples hardened to little stones. Dante ran his thumbs across them. She moaned. He enlisted his forefingers in the torment, pulling at those sweet peaks harder than he had before. She bucked against him, ramming their hips together, arching her back, and tearing a hand into his hair again. Her nails dug into his scalp, pulling his face into her neck. He took the pain gladly because it turned into a bolt of pure electricity by the time it shot to his cock.

"I take it you still want to stay, *stellina*?" He grazed her neck with his teeth and then laved the abrasion with his tongue. Her fervent nod clutched at his chest and filled his soul. It was more than enough for now. Forcing her to form words wasn't the goal this moment. Forcing her to see a new side of herself, a terrifying discovery in herself—that was the plan and the much harder mission. *Merda,* he'd spearheaded multimillion-dollar mergers with more confidence than his next step.

Luckily, Mark had walked him through a few key points. His friend's words resonated in his mind. *Listen to what her body tells you. Follow that with what your gut says.*

The trouble was, his gut wasn't doing the talking right now. The last time he'd endured a more painful erection, he'd been fifteen. Celina's urgent little hip rolls helped as much as tinfoil in a lightning storm. He clenched his jaw and reset his legs, setting them just inside hers. He put them there to support hers...or at least that was the bullshit he was going with the moment.

Go with his gut. Right, his gut. It was around here somewhere. He hoped.

"What else do you want?" The words felt good. And

they did generate from his gut, though this part of his instinct wasn't so familiar to him. It had only been awakened in full force on Friday and then taken out to examine in curious little chunks throughout the week. Mark had given him a name for it. His hidden Dom. He'd winced when his friend first slapped the term on him, but he now realized the label was fucking perfect. He liked this part of him. And he loved what it did to the woman in his arms.

"What else do you want, *cara*?" He ground even more command into the repetition, reveling in her deep shiver of reaction. "Do you want more of this?" He gripped her breasts fully, twisting the luscious skin and making her cry out. The sound ripped through him with primal force. "Do you like what the pain does to you?" He bit into her earlobe. "Do you like where it sends your mind, your body?"

She let out a louder shriek as he gave her mounds a pair of light swats. When he thumbed her nipples again, they were hot and pulsing.

"Yes," he whispered. "You do want it, don't you?"

She shook again. She was still a mess of deep confusion. He felt it in every undulation of her body, especially when things got more intense on the other side of the room. Mark tossed aside the crop and opted for a pair of long, heavy leather floggers. He gave Rose a kiss on the back of her neck before continuing to her ear, murmuring something that made his wife's body go limp in the cuffs. Then he backed up from her by three broad steps.

"Shit!"

The scream came from Rose as her Dom landed the flogger falls hard into her back. She gave the word a do-over when he crossed his arms and delivered a second strike, echoing the force of the first.

"Anything you'd like to contribute to this exchange besides that, pet?" Mark queried.

"N-No, Sir." It was tight yet breathy. Dante imagined the same two words coming out of Celina like that, and his erection beat at his pants like Satan's hammer.

Across the room, Mark went into an underhand motion, flicking the falls softly along Rose's pussy. "Your back looks amazing, my love."

"Thank you, Master."

"It's setting my cock on fire."

She sighed. "I'm glad, Master."

"Does it burn for you too, honey? Is your skin hot now?"

"Oh yes, Sir."

"A lot?"

She tilted a teasing glance. "Not *a lot...*"

"Pity."

Without warning, he swung the floggers in two more fierce overhands. The smacks literally rang off the walls. Mark kept up the strokes this time, whirling the floggers in graceful figure eights that crisscrossed each other on their way to his subbie's creamy back. Rose screamed. Celina wanted to. Dante could tell. He felt the strain in her muscles and the convulsion in her throat as she held back the exclamation.

"Stop holding it in," Dante ordered. "Goddammit, Celina, I need to know what you're feeling!"

Her hand dropped from his head, flailing helplessly. "I'm trying." Her voice broke, tugging at both his heart and his cock. "Oh God, I'm trying, but—"

"But what?"

Beneath his hands, her chest trembled as she struggled

for air. He felt her frustration, even related to it. This was a gigantic door to throw open to her at once, but Dante refused to acquiesce now. This was a fight, a quest for the prize of what they'd merely glimpsed Friday night. But she was having trouble accepting what she saw and felt as a "prize." He was dedicated to keeping the door open, to making her see differently.

Stunningly, the submissive across the room came to his rescue on that front.

With every kiss of the flogger to her skin, Rose Moore turned into a sexier little pet for her Master. Just as Celina wrestled with her answer for Dante, Rose's ordeal got the best of her. She twisted and shivered. Her head no longer lolled but thrashed. Her ass quivered, and her thighs trembled. "Master!" she shrieked. "Oh please!"

A grin parted Mark's lips. "Please what, pet?"

Rose huffed. Her buttocks constricted. "Master! I'm so close!"

"Don't you dare think it, Rose. Tighten that ass harder. Control your sweet, juicy pussy. No coming without my command, honey. We have guests. Make me proud."

Rose let loose a sound best described as pissed-off she-cat. "Damn it!"

Mark didn't help her frustration by letting out a chuckle. He brushed her back with taunting strokes of the flogger. "Honey." His voice dipped with reproach. "I'm going to give you what you need, right?"

The she-cat hiss became a soft moan. "Yes, Master."

"Well, I only want to hear you say it. Give me the words, Rose. Give them to me loud and clear. Show Dante's lovely lady what good subbies get when they face and then find the strength of their surrender." He gave the flogger strokes a little more strength. "What can Master give you? Tell me, Rosalind." He hit even more skin. He used even more force. "*Tell me*, pet!"

"Harder." Her whole body strained. "Please, my skin needs more. Harder! Please!"

"And why does your skin need more?"

"B-Because my spirit needs more. Ohhhh *yes*! Again!"

"Your spirit...and what else?"

"My—my body. My—my pussy. It—it—"

Rose faltered, interrupting with her own tearful sob. Celina grabbed Dante again. Her fingernails made crescents in his forearms. He didn't feel her breathe but couldn't take in air for himself either.

Thunk. Thunk.

Mark dropped both floggers and then stepped over them to his wife. With the surety of the soldier who still stomped through his bloodstream, he twirled her on the cuff chains so she faced him again. Nearly in the same movement, he slid a hand past the mahogany curls at her apex. His other arm bunched as he caught her, holding her steady for his invasion into her core.

"Give it to me, pet." It was a gritted mix of conquest and request. "Shatter for me, love. Now!"

"Yes, Sir." She gasped. "Yes, Sir. Oh...yesssssssssss!"

While Rose Moore climaxed into a billion shards for her Master, Mark unlatched her from the suspension cuffs and extended her orgasm by gripping her hips and rubbing her pussy against the huge ridge in his crotch. Her breaths slammed out of her in time to that rhythm. She gripped his shoulders like he was driftwood in a hurricane.

Celina's own breath kept the same beat. Dante knew

because she had him nearly wrapped around her now, his hands clutched between her breasts and her hips wedged between his. Beneath his palms, her heartbeat was a stampede. Under his pants, his cock was an inferno. He locked his knees to keep on standing, discovering it got a little easier to tamp his lust if he focused on keeping her stable.

That became damn near impossible as Rose's sighs started pitching toward ecstasy again.

"No," came Mark's strict command. "Don't do it, Rose. Don't you dare!"

"Fuck!" Rose screamed. "Master! Ahhhh!"

With a whimper of defeat, the woman in Dante's arms crumbled to her knees. They were so tangled with each other, he fell with her. "Easy, *stellina*. I've got you. Easy."

"Easy?" she snapped. *"Eísai trelós?* This isn't easy, damn it!"

"I'm completely sane, *cara*—and of course I know this isn't easy." Now that he had better leverage, he tucked his head tighter against her neck. "But we're here doing this together. I'm right here. I want to give you everything you crave, show you everything you can be." He breathed in deeply, loving the eucalyptus scent of her shampoo, the tang of sweat on her skin, the heady hint of her arousal. "Fuck," he whispered. "You feel so good. You've been so good tonight. So right..."

He spilled it all into her ear as Mark tilted his head and murmured more things to Rose that he couldn't hear. But as Celina melted deeper against him, he concluded the guy could be reciting the Declaration of Independence for all he cared. His pulse hammered harder when his *stellina* pulled his hands back up to her breasts, coaxing him to pinch her there again.

"Make me feel even more right," she whispered.

"P-Please?"

He hesitated for a second, feeling around for his elusive gut. Once again, the only thing operating at full volume was the megaphone of his cock. But damn it, tonight wasn't about getting inside her body. He needed to open her *mind*, and he had to do that before she bolted. He'd barely expected her to honor a full hour in here. He sure as hell hadn't predicted she'd beg to stay.

And this turn? This belonged so far in the realm of his dreams, he had no idea what to do now.

"Dante. Oh God, Dante!"

Her urgent rasp coincided with the trip Mark took across the room now, his naked wife still clinging to him. His stare was already fixed on the leather bondage swing. He settled Rose in it and then shackled her. The woman now lay open for her Master, legs apart, arms over her head, her body bent in a soft V, and a look of pure longing on her face. Every blink of her eyes riveted her gaze harder on Mark. Her chest rose and fell in a feverish pace as he stripped off his shirt and then moved between her thighs.

"What do you need from me now, Rose?"

Dante tightened his fingers on Celina's nipples, a silent version of the same question.

"Please, Master...your cock. Fill me with your cock!"

Celina gave her own answer by taking one of Dante's hands and jamming it down the front of her skirt.

"Fuck, yes." Mark exclaimed it as he let down his zipper and palmed his full erection.

"Fuck, *yes.*" Dante's version of it came from the part of him that could still talk. The other part only churned a wordless snarl as his fingers dipped into the heaven of wet, soft layers at the apex of Celina's thighs. A small distraction came from the material now grating against his forearm. It took a second to recognize the texture and then another for the insight to shoot its way to his cock.

"Holy shit," he uttered. "You're wearing fishnets?"

She gave a guilty-as-charged smile, which should've meant some tension relief for them both. It only cranked the pressure in his body even tighter. He needed to possess this woman every way he could. She captivated him more with every second they spent together. All the surprising moments like this. All her embarrassed little looks. All the revelations of a sexuality she'd barely explored, all unveiled beneath his fingers, at his will.

Oh, who the fuck was he kidding?

She was the one exposing *him*. Uncovering him. Awakening him.

He was in trouble here.

But it was the best damn trouble of his life.

As his mind tumbled with that thought, his free hand curled into the hem of her skirt. He rammed the garment up from the back. *Porca vacca.* The swells of her backside were so sweet and full, accented in all the right ways by the mesh of the stockings and the naughty slit of her black satin thong. Goddamn it—fishnets *and* black satin? On top of the hold she secured again to his scalp, anchoring his body along hers? His prim little JAG was turning this risk of a night into one hell of a sensual shock.

Across the room, Mark grabbed the leather loops at the sides of Rose's head. He pulled the whole swing forward, impaling his subbie's body onto his cock. "Ready for the ride, honey?" he asked as she moaned.

Dante felt the responding shudder claim Celina's body. Swift about it now, he pulled back her labia with a couple of fingers and then stroked two more along her most sensitive band of flesh. She quivered and emitted the sexiest mewl he'd ever heard. Dante growled low and bit her neck. "Ready for the ride, *stellina*?"

CHAPTER TWELVE

No. No, she wasn't ready!

The protest careened through Celina's mind like a derailed roller-coaster car. Appropriate image. Her mind, her body, and her senses were on a ride of dipping, speeding confusion.

She was respectable, for God's sake. Dutiful. She did productive things with her life. She was a devoted naval officer, an attentive legal advocate, a fighter for justice. She planned the family picnics and took her niece to Six Flags every summer. She *didn't* do things like play voyeur in secret bondage clubs and then beg her playboy party host to get her off while—

"Ohhhhh!"

But that's exactly what Dante was hell-bent on accomplishing. The raw need in her wail testified to that.

"Dante. Oh God, we can't—"

"Hush." His mandate was a harsh sough in her ear. He backed it with a small smack at her thigh. "Hang on tight. Watch them...and feel me."

Just as he ordered it, her stare locked on Rose Moore's face. The woman's lips were a curve of pure joy. Her gaze showered her husband in complete adoration. Her body glowed as her Master drove into her again and again, crooning words of praise as he filled her, completed her.

It was one of the most incredible things she'd ever seen.

Dante's touch was one of the most exquisite things she'd ever felt.

She moaned as he rolled his hips against her in the same cadence Mark set. Deep in her pussy, his fingers matched the beat in relentless, remorseless thrusts. He hadn't removed a shred of his clothes and didn't try to get her any further out of hers—a factor that only made this feel more illicit, forbidden, a dream of catastrophic proportions.

"My *stellina*." He pushed into her more urgently.

"My sweet pet," Mark uttered to Rose.

"Come for me, Celina!"

"Come for me, Rose!"

There wasn't any buildup to the eruption. Celina lost her breath from the shock of it as Rose's scream filled the room from hers. In ten seconds, her body revved from freeway velocity to light speed. The climax pulled her mind outside her skull, spinning her, carrying her, terrifying her. She clung to Dante as her only anchor in the whirl, convulsing his fingers tighter into her pussy and gripping his hair hard in her hand.

"Fuck!" The word burst from him in a hot explosion on her neck.

"Fuck!" Mark exclaimed as he pumped the swing hard. As he froze, clearly spilling himself inside his wife, Dante seized and shuddered at Celina's back.

For many minutes, nobody in the room spoke. As if they could. After they were all sucked so high into the cosmos, air seemed nonexistent. With slow tenderness, Mark unbuckled Rose from the swing's restraints and then scooted into the sling with her. He pulled her into his arms and started kissing her cheeks and forehead. She'd started to cry, not that Celina blamed her. Everything in her body wanted to crumble to the floor and do the same thing, but she gritted her teeth and battled the sentiment. Falling apart was definitely not the right follow-up here. She wasn't quite sure what was, but instinct started backing her soul up out of the room already, even if her body couldn't yet find the strength.

The admission did nothing to help her accept Dante's next move. He stood and then scooped her into his arms before she could form a rational thought.

"Dante, really, I can walk on my—"

"Hush." He swiped his lips across her forehead as he paused in front of the door to their private room. While balancing on one leg, he pushed down the door's latch with the other foot. For a second, she wondered if he'd been a circus freak in another life. The man was muscled grace on two legs. He proved her more right as he kicked the door shut and then moved to the couch, settling her firmly on his lap.

"Dante—"

"Hush," he repeated, taking her lips under his. He lingered with the kiss, though it was far from an attack. It felt more like an affirmation...

But of what?

Answers to that dived at her brain like marauding F-18s. What *was* going to happen now? This had changed things between them; there was no doubt about that. But that was the bubbling core of the reactor too. There wasn't supposed to be any "them."

Crap. She hadn't asked for any of this. He'd ambushed her, even gotten her two best "friends" to help him do it, and then pulled her into a world she thought only existed in her brothers' wildest fantasies...

Which apparently were her fantasies too.

You begged him to let you stay, Cel. Even after your hour was up.

A conflicted whimper tore up her throat. Dante released her mouth, though he lifted a hand and stroked her cheek.

"You okay?" His voice was as careful as his touch. He reached across the couch. A blanket had magically appeared there, during their time in what she'd secretly dubbed the Den of Decadence. With gentle tugs, he wrapped her naked torso with it.

"I..." she muttered. "I, uh—yeah, I'm fine."

"Why don't I believe you?" An ironic smile parted his dark beard. "You're trembling, *stellina*."

She shrugged. "I'm just a little cold."

He snuggled her closer to his chest. He was as toasty as a furnace. A bar-bully-kicking, Cirque-balancing, orgasm-inducing furnace. Crap, maybe money could buy everything.

No. Not everything. Not her.

She pulled away a little and dropped her gaze into her lap.

"Talk to me, Celina."

He spoke in the same tone he'd used back in the den. Ordering, not asking.

"Talk? About what?"

"About *what*?" He chuffed. "Well, just a thought. Let's start with what happened over the last ninety minutes, yeah?"

She twisted her fingertips together. "What about them?"

He let out a long breath and then quietly questioned, "Did you like them?"

"I—" She looked back up, hoping the indigo-and-black layers of his eyes would wrest words from her. Instead, a question bloomed in her mind and then burned at her lips. "Did *you* like them? I mean, did you—were you able to—"

"Come?" He chuckled, biting his bottom lip a little. Her stomach did a funny flip. Okay yeah, she loved the lip-biting thing. "Yes, *cara*. The last ninety minutes have been pretty great for me. Don't worry." He raised his palm to her cheek again. "But we were talking about you. Address the question, please."

Now curiosity really flamed. "Okay, but why didn't you—" Her cheeks joined the club, burning to the backs of her eye sockets. "Well, why did you have us stay like that, then? With our clothes on? Why not—"

"Are you going to answer my question?"

"Are you going to answer mine?" she retorted. "Why the clothes?"

His black brows lowered, but his eyes softened to dark charcoal. "Did you want to be totally naked? Did the clothes make things bad for you?"

All right, forget the lip biting. That look, a mixture of complete control and concern in the same moment, turned the gut flips into full cartwheels. She took his hand, tangling her fingers with his. Hell, she was actually worried about giving him a wrong impression. Which wasn't a huge sin, right? Wasn't it natural to be a *little* concerned about a guy after he turned you into a billion pieces of ecstasy?

"It was the most amazing thing my body's ever experienced."

And my mind. And my soul.

His Roman lips parted on a soft smile. "Yeah," he murmured. "Mine too."

The man could be bigger than life in so many ways but had never enraptured her more than this moment as he bent his head and feathered that luscious mouth over hers. He pulled back by a few inches before speaking again. "The clothes stayed on, *cara,* because I didn't bring you here tonight to have sex with you." He held up a hand. "*Lo giuro sulla mia bibbia della nonna morta.* It's the truth!"

She slapped his shoulder. "*Morta?* Did you just invoke a dead person to make your point?"

"My *nonna* wouldn't mind." He still smiled with that, though his eyes sobered. "What we have, Celina...what we've discovered with each other—this is about more than sex. I know it; you know it. If it had been about a few hours of crazy passion, we both would've been able to walk away."

"I wasn't 'walking' that well last Saturday," she grumbled, enjoying his answering chuckle.

"At least you remembered me." Once more, the tone was light, but his mien shifted to shadows. He dipped a finger beneath her chin and pulled her face up. "I couldn't stop thinking about you." He kissed her softly again. "I'll tell you that a million more times if I have to. I'm not ashamed of it. I'm not ashamed of *us.*" His hand slid down her neck under the blanket and around her shoulder. "I know this is fast. I know this is overwhelming. But this is also *right.* It's so right..."

He kissed her with more hunger now, dipping his tongue along hers and tugging at her lip with his teeth between his deep plunges. Celina's body turned into a mass of needy magma that oozed over the landscape of her logic. Holy crap, could the man kiss. Her heart thudded with arousal and terror combined. He was right. This was overwhelming. And she had no idea what to do.

"So," he finally murmured, "in answer to your question, the next time I get naked with you, I want it to count. I want it to count a lot. I want it to mean something."

The magma kept coming. The confusion did too. Celina pushed from his hold, clutching the blanket with one hand

and scraping back her hair with the other. Though she now sat just a foot away from him, the couch's cushions felt cold in comparison to his body.

"Dante, I'm not sure there should be a next time."

She expected his thick tension. Perhaps a minute or two of his silence. But when the stillness went on, turning the room from a plush haven into something more like a sepulchre, she wound her fingers together again. From the moment she'd met the man, the force of his spirit could dominate a football stadium. Now she couldn't sense a single emotion from him. An ice bath would've been less jarring.

Dante rose in one quiet motion. He opened the door into the play den again, shutting it with barely a click. Half a minute later, he came back bearing her bra and turtleneck. Her sweater was a tangle. He patiently pulled it apart before draping it across the easy chair's arm. He draped the bra on top of it.

"I'm going to clean up." His voice was low and flat. The words ripped into Celina as if he'd screamed them.

"Dante—"

Another *click* of the door answered her. This time it was the bathroom's portal. The bathroom fan turned on. She heard his zipper slide down, the splash of water hitting a washcloth, the rustle of his clothes, but still nothing from him. Strangely, tears pricked her eyes. She gritted them away, searching for a surge of pissed to throw into the stupid pit of sentiment.

"What did you expect, Cel?" she muttered.

What *did* she expect? She shook as her brain tiptoed toward the answer. And, if she was being honest, as her heart did too. Everything about tonight had taken her mental box marked *Relationships* and dumped the damn thing across the floor of her psyche. She'd watched a beautiful, headstrong woman submit to her Dom and liked it. *Really* liked it. She'd begged the man *she* was with for fulfillment and loved it. She'd imagined herself as that submissive...and God help her, she'd longed for Dante as her Dom. Dante Tieri, the epitome of Mr. *Not* Right on every page of her rule book. Dante Tieri, who could buy off any woman in the state but decided to turn *her* world into goulash instead.

Dante, who'd fought for her at the Blue Sax.

Dante, who called her his star.

Dante, who'd arranged everything tonight just to explore all this by her side, who had the guts to open himself to it too.

She didn't know what to do now. She didn't know what to feel.

"Damn it!" The desperation in her voice filled the room. With frustrated jerks, she reached for her bra and managed to get it on right. The turtleneck was another story. With her eyes smarting, her lips quavering, and her muscles still turned into rubber bands, she tried to pull it on but ended up with her head stuck in a sleeve and one arm out the neck. "Fucking hell!"

Two strong hands pulled the thing off her. Her skirmish with the top had drowned out Dante's reentry to the room. Now inches away once more, he righted the turtleneck, bunching up the fabric to push it over her head.

Her gaze lifted to his.

His hands froze.

Her heart clutched around the breath she held, the anticipation she endured. She watched the dark depths of his eyes, so intent beneath his ink-dark lashes. Any minute now, he was going to hurl the sweater to the couch, haul her close to him again, and use his lips—and his touch and his hips and anything else he had at his disposal—to shove all her doubts out of her again. And God help her, she couldn't wait.

With a heavy exhalation, he lifted the sweater over her head.

As the material cleared her face, Celina stared up at him. She fought down the fire in her arms, the burning lust to hold him again. She pressed her lips together to hold in the entreaty that scratched and screamed for a way out.

Hold me. Please. Just one more time before I have to get out of here.

She shivered, huddling her arms against her chest, though her thumbs knocked her sternum like dual ice picks. Despite that, there was no way she was hurrying into the damn sweater. If he wanted to help her get dressed so badly, he could work for the privilege. But she couldn't tell anything by looking at his face. He still seemed switched to automatic pilot. The gears were working, but the life in him was gone.

At last, a tiny wince crossed his brow. For a flicker of a moment, he was back. His gaze was heated like smoldering coal. His mouth parted as if he was very hungry and she'd turned into a plate of homemade pasta. Appropriate, since everything from her scalp to her toes felt like a gigantic moist noodle.

He lifted both his hands, as if to grab the turtleneck's arms. Instead, he caressed the lengths of hers. It was only his knuckles, but they were like stones warmed in Tuscan sun. Celina gritted her jaw to keep her sigh in. *Skata,* that resolve lasted for three seconds. In shuddering spurts, her breath left her.

With slow intent, Dante leaned closer. He captured the last of her exhalations with his lips. If his fingers were the warmth of Tuscany, his mouth was the temptation of Rome—and she craved more. God yes, more. As her head fought the thought, her body surrendered to it. She lifted her face, wordlessly begging him to open her again, to conquer her again. But with every inch she pressed closer, Dante pulled back. He was rigid with tension from the effort, but he wouldn't touch her any deeper than this, as if she really were that overcooked pasta and he was afraid of disintegrating her.

His head dipped as he dragged away with a hard swallow. He scooped one hand to her nape. A misty smile graced his lips.

"*Stellina,* I've done everything I can to show you what this can be, what we can have together. I want this. With you. *Only* you. But I can't order the 'yes' from your lips. I can't grab the power from your hands."

He stepped back but circled both her wrists in his grip. Celina frowned. After the words he'd just issued, the move didn't make sense, until he turned both her hands over. Into the center of each of her palms, he pressed a quiet kiss. When he looked up again, his gaze was again impenetrable onyx.

"It's all here now, *cara.* The decision is yours." He lifted those warm knuckles to her cheek. "Thanksgiving is in five days. You'd be the perfect blessing for which to bow my head at the feasting table."

His words, sounding like a prayer already, swirled into her like smoke off a thousand votive candles and drowned her breath just as completely. When he slipped his hand from her skin, all the candles blew out. Everything was cold once again. Pure instinct compelling her, she reached for him, but he'd already turned. Half a dozen steps, broad and determined, took him to the outer door.

Then he was gone.

She sank onto the couch again. She wondered why she felt like sobbing. She tried to give in to the temptation at last, but her teeth started to chatter instead.

★ ★ ★

She blamed the ongoing chill on the turn the weather had taken. She stayed in all day Sunday with the furnace blasting, her e-reader in her lap, and her phone at her side. She got a dozen texts from Sami, a few from Dylan, and even one from Nik, who sent his best from the Middle Eastern desert as he got ready to go prevent something else from going boom. And Cameron? She didn't expect to hear from him for several weeks. SEAL training pretty much shot a guy's family time to zero.

Not a single call or text from Dante.

Not that she allowed herself to notice. For longer than a minute at a time.

Not that she didn't tell herself a thousand times that she lived in the world of reality, not fantasy—that the "decision" he'd put back in her hands was one that didn't involve just her, and running off to Oz was fine if someone was an eighteen-year-old with no integrity, responsibility, or family. Especially if that someone's family hadn't been torn apart twice by the flash of a black Amex and its matching Jag. Especially if that someone's three naval officer brothers wouldn't be jumping on said Jag owner's ass—and God only knew what else—for being a sister-stealing old man as well. She wished she could be even half kidding about that scenario, but she could predict her brothers better than the Doppler foretold the rain. Maybe Dante wasn't eighty, but he was at least half that, far away enough from her twenty-nine that Dyl, Nik, and Cam would be pulling out the black scowls and the invisible *Rejected* stamps faster than she could finish family introductions.

It was better this way.

It had to be better this way.

She'd forget about how good it all felt...soon. She'd be back to normal...eventually. She'd stop looking at her phone every five minutes...tomorrow.

She told herself all those things as Sunday night turned into Monday morning and then was on the verge of merging into Monday afternoon. But by now, she was beyond "telling" it all. As she stood in the bathroom at work staring at herself in the mirror, she promoted her inner mantra guru into a seething drill sergeant.

"Get your act together, Celina. He's stepped away, and you're fine with that. He's given you the choice, and you've made it. And it's the right one. It's the *right one*."

She just needed to ignore the pretzel twist of her gut and the frozen slush of her heart that said otherwise.

With her stomach aching from that metaphysical junk-food fest, she splashed water on her face then, prepared to jam her phone into her purse for the rest of the day.

Just before she let go, her screen flashed with a text.

It was from Eve, which was a surprise. Things hadn't been hearts and flowers with her friend since the night of the big party, and they'd gotten more strained after she'd rejoined her friends at Trev's birthday party, only to park herself against a wall as she'd tried to sort out the events from Dark Escape. Eve had taken one look at Celina's tangled hair and wrinkled sweater, jumped to the naughtiest conclusion possible, and assumed herself forgiven for the secret scheming with Dante.

When that didn't earn her a full disclosure of what had happened, the previous frost on her demeanor had turned into an ice front, especially during the case review meeting this morning.

Her friend's text seemed a small attempt at a truce, not so much for its brevity as its punctuation.

PFG needs to see you. ☺

She blinked at the screen and wondered why their commander was hunting for her. Case review had ended just an hour ago; all her files were in order. Nerves spurring her pace, she made her way to the office marked *Commander George Threshan*. Eve, Reiley, and she privately called him PFG for short because "George" just didn't cut it when matched to the man's six-and-a-half-foot frame, piercing blue eyes, and sinfully thick blond hair, even tamed in its military cut. Three days after he'd transferred here, "Prince Fucking Gorgeous" had been conceived over a giggly lunch hour. "PFG" had come soon after.

Celina gave a polite knock to the door frame. "Commander? I heard you were looking for me."

The man looked up from the mountain of files on his desk. His eyebrows jumped. "Commander? What the hell, Cel?" He lifted a disarming grin. "Do you think you're in trouble or something?"

She let out a breath. "Actually, that's exactly what I thought."

"Knock it off. Right now. And get your ass in here, counselor." He rose and crossed to a small round conference table, pulling out a chair for her too. Celina again indulged a musing common to all the women in the office. Why wasn't this guy, who could be David Beckham's older brother, out raking in a small fortune on a bunch of fashion runways and film sets?

She only had a few seconds to indulge the thought before Threshan scooted the door closed with one foot. "Okay," she ventured, "are you *sure* I'm not in trouble?"

He balanced on the back two legs of his own chair, steepling his fingers. "It's about Zell and Zach Braden."

Her heartbeat spiked. Not trouble. Something worse. "What about them? Are they okay?" Just as fast, the somber look on PFG's face hit her. "Crap. What's Cassandra pulled now?" She almost expected him to chuckle, but when he didn't, her pulse sprinted again. "Damn it! It *is* that bitch! What's she done?"

Threshan gave her half a minute to get calm before scooting a thick file toward her. "Braden's civilian team obtained this yesterday. It's the contract for her reality show. TruBlu Productions hasn't signed yet. That's because there's a little contingency clause to their go-ahead on the deal."

Her throat went tight with fury. "Zach," she spat. "She has to have full custody of Zach, or they won't do the show."

"B-I-N-G-O."

She fought the urge to rip the folder in half. "Over my dead and rotting body."

Threshan chuffed. "Sorta thought you'd say that. It's why that file also contains the official clearance papers for you to follow this thing to Tokyo. Fill it all out. I'll sign it and send it up the chain. Sure hope you like rice, Cel."

A confused frown hit her. "Wait. Zach is an American citizen. Why the hell is Zell fighting this on their turf?"

"It's where we have to start. Apparently, Cassandra got some kind of 'special permission' to do it in a 'neutral court' there, approved by both sides. But I need *you* there, Cel. This is going to be a delicate public-relations feat. This Cassandra is a real piece of loose-lipped work."

Celina snorted. "Gee, you think?"

"Brace yourself. There's more."

"*What?*"

"She already got one of the major Japanese tabloids to run a story about her 'soldier ex-husband with the insane temper,' who's now supposedly ripped her sweet little boy from her side and won't let her see him at all."

"That...little..." The depth of her fury cut her short. She watched her skin go white against her knuckles as she coiled a fist against the table. "Does the woman have room to move in that mound of bullshit around her? Zell Braden has had nothing but patience with that woman. Or maybe all the henna in her hair has finally fried her brain."

"Which is why she's so at home with the Japanese gossip press, I suppose."

The anger intensified. Celina almost welcomed it. For the first time in ten days, she was completely clear about her emotions for something. Rage wouldn't have been her first choice for the feat, but it was, in many ways, a comfort. She thought of Zach Braden, a dark-haired cutie who shared his father's love for laughter and cheeseburgers, and the concept of him as a prize for a TV deal made her flesh crawl.

"When does this thing get going?" she demanded. "And how long should I plan to be there?"

Threshan's initial reply was an oddly quiet stare. He collapsed his finger steeple but kept his indexes pressed like a pistol. "That's an interesting pair of questions."

She stared at him. "What do you mean?"

The man's gaze now held the intensity of a July sky. "In answer to part one, you can take your time packing, Lieutenant. You're only there for support and advice for Braden, not as actual counsel. I know you won't forget that, right?"

"Of course not. But I appreciate you making it happen so I can be there. Zell's going to need all the support he can get."

"Oh, yeah."

"So when do I go?"

"Easy there, Dirty Harry. Thanksgiving is in three days. The holidays are here. They're not going to get into any of this until January. Cassandra can squeal all the way to our commander-in-chief if she wants, but Zach will be stateside with Zell until after New Year's, at least."

She whooshed out a breath. "Thank God."

"Now as for your question, part two..." He tilted his head, hitting her with tighter scrutiny. "That's a more complicated issue."

Celina frowned again. "Complicated how?"

"Late yesterday, I was on the line about the case with the commander for Japan Region Legal. He's damn grateful for your work on this case so far, Cel."

She looked away, unsure of the intent she sensed in her commander's voice, trying to dim the spidey sense with a deprecating laugh. "Well, he won't be so impressed if Zach Braden ends up dating a Harajuku girl at the age of ten in the name of a ratings boost."

"He doesn't think that's going to happen."

"I'm going to make damn sure it doesn't."

"I know." He brought the chair back to four legs with a resigned *thump*. "And he does too. Which is why you've landed solid in the middle of his radar."

So much for squashing the spidey sense. It glowed like a tarantula's web under black light. "His radar," Celina said. "You mean his *big* radar? As in long-term-reassignment radar?"

"He's in shitty shape for good JAs, Celina." He shook his head and winced. "I'd fucking hate to lose you, but it's a hell of an opportunity to make a difference to the folks who are serving there, even if you only go for six months. Nobody's had it easy in Japan since the tsunami. That all said, it's a great place for an assignment. A truly beautiful land."

She managed to nod as her mind spun again. A beautiful land. Well, that much was certain. It was also an amazing chance to serve, a true adventure.

It was also nearly six thousand miles from home.

She huffed at that attack of mush. Since when had she, Dad, and the guys ever gotten stupid about that stuff? They were the Kouris clan. Four generations of military service and counting. "Home" could be a tent on a godforsaken cliff somewhere, as long as they were all together.

But it's also six thousand miles away from Dante Tieri.

It was a blessing and a curse in one sentence. She struggled to embrace the former and ignore the latter. Hell. What part of "perfect gift from destiny" wasn't she getting about this? Wasn't this the space she desperately needed from him? The challenge of a new position and the wonder of a new land... They were the ideal eraser for all the tumult of the last ten days. This was exactly the push she needed for closing the door in her life with his name on it...for good. Dylan and Sami could help Dad mind her house for six months. Eve and Rei would *not* complain about an excuse to come to Japan and see her. She'd even be a little closer to Nik, not that her workaholic, bomb-defusing brother ever took significant time off. There were at least a dozen other items that quickly wrote themselves into her mental plusses column.

All she had to do was give Threshan one word of an answer.

CHAPTER THIRTEEN

"Dante? Dante? *Lei ascolta, regazzo?*"

"Yes, *Mamma*. I'm listening." He looked out over the city lights, becoming increasingly fuzzy through the thickening clouds outside the window, from his massive velour couch. Why had he let his designer talk him into cream for a color? Why had he let her get something so huge?

No, not huge.

The cushions felt empty.

Like his days and nights had felt since Sunday.

He took another swig of Scotch and scowled. On the stereo, his "morosity music mix" restarted itself. Johnny Cash started singing about needles and broken thoughts. After him, the Eagles, Bob Dylan, Radiohead, and Billie Holiday would have their turns at the hit parade of depression.

Get the fuck over it. She's not going to call. You tried to open her baggage; she threw the locks on and tossed the key. Congratulations, man. You found the one woman on the globe who thinks your money is filthy, your touch is tainted, your experience is a liability, and even your jokes are half-good at best. Add the whole revelation about your Dominance to the mix, and no wonder she's moved the hell on.

Suck it up. It's time for you to move on too.

Why the hell was that so much easier said than done?

"So you will come tomorrow for dinner, *si*? Dante?"

"Yeah, Mom. Of course. I'm doing the meatballs again

too. Tell Marzi I'm doing an extra-spicy batch for her."

A cluck came over the line. "*Merda.* That sister of yours. The *bambino* make her stomach a soccer ball for the spicy food, *sì*?"

He chuckled. "She's only four months along, *Mamma.* Give the kid a chance to grow legs before she starts to kick her."

"*He.* Before *he* starts to kick," she corrected. "A beautiful baby boy for me to love, since my two are now gone..."

He pinched his nose between two fingers and begged at least three saints for patience. She got this way at holidays. The wine came out for cooking, and his thoroughly Italian mother didn't know how to stop. "Raff and I aren't gone, *Mamma.*"

"No? When was the last time you heard from Raffaele, eh?"

He grimaced from the invisible corner into which he'd just shoved himself. The shitty thing was, the question was valid. Since Arianne's self-inspired dive off a Paris balcony two years ago, his brother had decided sanity could hit the pavement too. Raff had elevated the game of globe-trotting-do-nothing lady snack to a thoroughly smutty art form now, and it was breaking their mother's heart.

"I'll be there, *Mamma,*" he emphasized. "And we'll all have a nice time, okay?"

He got a heavy sniff in reply. "Fine, fine. But you no fool me, Dante. Your heart is far away now too."

He got to his feet. Like doing *that* was going to help him escape the woman's laser-accurate insight, even from across town. How the hell did she do that? "I'm fine, *Mamma.* Don't focus on me." *Please don't.*

"It is this Celina, *sì*? I like her when I talk to her. You bring her tomorrow, *agori mou*?"

It was definitely time for more Scotch.

"Uhhh...no. Sorry, she—"

A series of chimes interrupted his words as well as his walk to the wet bar. It was the call line from the Elysian's security desk. He frowned in curiosity as he switched direction and headed to the flat panel that would connect him to the lobby, forty-five floors below. As he did, he plunked down his glass in the kitchen.

When he punched on the screen, he was glad he didn't have the glass anymore. He was sure he would've dropped it.

"*Mamma,* I need to go. I'll see you tomorrow." Before he disconnected the phone, he jammed on the intercom to Gilles at the security desk. "Let her up."

On the video screen, he watched Celina's huddled form hurry off to the elevator.

At the foyer of his floor, he cursed the thing three times for not moving fast enough.

That was a good thing, perhaps. Yeah, best to remember that his tongue could actually function—right before he swallowed it.

The big bomber jacket and thick scarf she'd had on in the lobby were now wrapped across her arms. What he expected to see beneath them... *Fuck.* It just wasn't this. He thanked the fashion gods for conceiving the wraparound dress concept, because it was perfect for this woman. Her slender curves were enfolded in sleeveless dark-crimson velvet that was held together by a Byzantine-influenced brooch at her waist. The pattern was repeated in a bracelet thing she'd scooted around a bicep, as well as a necklace that fell perfectly into her cleavage. The dress fell to the tops of the boots she'd worn on Saturday night.

He had to be dreaming. He was still back in her house on the couch, and this was all a teasing fantasy, about to *poof* when he snored and woke himself up. That was why he couldn't talk. Yeah, that was it. He'd been born babbling, damn it. Words just didn't beat feet from his brain like this.

He stopped stressing about conversation when he looked deeper at her face. Her eyes were in enchanted-forest mode tonight, full of mossy shadows and deep thoughts, enhanced by a little makeup at their corners and on their lashes. She tried, unsuccessfully, not to chew at her lightly glossed lips. She pressed them together as she swallowed hard and tried to smile.

"Hi." Her greeting, while soft, bounced back from the white marble floor and walls. "I found your address on one of your old texts."

He smiled as warmth surged his chest again. "Then I'm glad I sent it so many times."

"I—I'm intruding." Her gaze did a nervous sweep around the foyer. She looked at the modern stone art busts like they were gargoyles about to come to life. "I should have called first. But I would've lost my nerve."

"It's okay." He issued it fast and got his hand around her back even faster. He hated that his world made her so skittish, but her confession was a good sign. She'd gotten dressed up for him. Gotten nervous about him. "Come on." He cupped his hand around her shoulder. Along with the hope, every protective instinct roared to life in him again too. "It's cold out here. Let me get you something." *Let me get you anything.*

She took a few visible breaths as he led her into his place, took her jacket, and laid it on the football field couch. Through all the motions, he didn't let her go. Though he was increasingly convinced she wasn't a hallucination, it was still best not to leave anything to chance. He let his hand drop into hers and pulled her toward the bar. The deeper he got her into the room, the better.

"You're freezing," he said. "It's going to snow tonight, I think." He splashed some Scotch into a fresh glass. "Sip this carefully. It'll warm you up." He brushed a strand of hair from her face as she complied and then grimaced from the strong liquor. Despite the wet air outside, her hair looked glorious. He fought the temptation to bury his hands in the shiny sable mane.

An awkward pause took over the air between them. This time, he didn't know how to interpret it.

"Dante, I came to see you..." She bit her lip again and turned to sit on the couch. That was before she stopped and gasped at the expansive view. "I—I had to see you—"

"It's okay. Go slow. I'm not going anywhere." He forced himself to stay next to the bar. Whatever she was trying to get out, she clearly needed some space to do so. He took another sip of Scotch himself, hoping it would loosen the Gordian knot now calling itself his gut.

She said her next words to the floor. "I haven't been able to stop thinking about Saturday night."

He swallowed hard. His body's first reaction, besides the rush of blood between his thighs, was to drive a fist into the air. But the quaver in her voice and her fascination with his wool carpet kept the emotional confetti cannons in check.

"I haven't either." He kept his voice modulated. "You were amazing. So brave for me. Thank you."

"You're welcome. It was...eye-opening for me too."

"In good ways?"

"In many ways."

She squirmed, almost like her own skin was too tight. Dante took a step toward her, but she stood and walked closer to the windows. Looking out into the mist and the lights, she continued, "I've landed at a crossroads because of it, on a couple of different levels. I don't know how you're going to feel about any of this, but I can't ignore that your feelings matter to me now."

He felt like throwing back the sliding door and taking a walk out on the balcony railing. It would've been less risky than the direction of her words. "Thanks," he muttered. "I think."

"Stop it," she snapped. "This is hard for me!"

He clenched his teeth. "I know."

"No," she countered. "I don't think you do."

She wheeled around, taking in the spacious room again and then shaking her head. To his eyes, it was simply a place to live, a living space he threw together for the sake of appearance for the corporation's stockholders. But he saw what it looked like to her. A damn palace. An extravagance for a prince with his head in the clouds. Literally.

"Do you know how hard it was for me to come here? To know it was shit like all of this that lured my mom away from my dad, from my family, and then ripped us all up again when Natalie left my brother? But I came, Dante, because of you. Because despite how I try, I can't forget you or how incredible it is to be with you. And I came because I know that will never change, even if GRI goes bankrupt tomorrow."

"Nor will how I feel about you." He didn't say it with any joy because he didn't feel any yet. The tormented lines of her face told him she still had plenty to confess, and most of it wouldn't be making its way onto a screen saver with hearts and butterflies.

"But even being with you is complicated now. I know you meant well on Saturday night, but all of that only crystallized things for me."

He forced himself to sit. An instinct told him it might put her a little more at ease, if that was a possibility right now. "I'm listening," he ensured her.

She twisted her fingers together. "And I'm here and confused." After a hard breath and a nervous glance, she started to pace. "You started it by saving my shit in that brawl at the Blue Sax. Then you didn't just put me in the cab, but you saw me home, personally—"

"*Stellina,*" he interjected. "That was the fun part."

"Yes, smartass, I get that. But then I woke up the next morning, thinking you'd probably left, to find you on the phone with your mom, to whom you'd just sent six dozen flowers."

"Not exactly following you. Wasn't that the point where we fought?"

"But you didn't let that stop you."

He smirked. "I guess you could say that."

To his shock, she gave a tiny smile in return. "All right, so the calls and the texts were a little weird. But sweet."

He let both eyebrows leap. "Sweet?"

"Own it, Tieri. It fits." Her smile dipped into serious territory again as her eyes gained an intense backlight. "It's part of why, as hard as I fought to keep it slapped on, you tore off that 'Hi, I'm Asshole Billionaire' name tag and burned it right out of my fingers."

He let his brows drop in perplexity. "That's a good thing, right?"

"Not when you're the woman who dreams of the lights going out and that sweet guy turning into a Dark Escape Dom."

The words clung to the air between them, thicker than the clouds outside the window. Elation cut through it, beaming into Dante's senses. "Celina—"

"That's insane, right?" She spread her hands, shaking her head. "How can I ask for a man to be two things? How can I want the man with flowers in one hand and a flogger in the other? This is the twenty-first century. I'll be thirty in six months. I'm supposed to be evolved! I'm supposed to know what I want! How can I be so confused about this?"

Dante lurched back to his feet. He grabbed her hands in his own and jammed them against her sides while he pressed close. She had to lean back to keep looking at him, a position that did some crazy, amazing things to his arousal level.

"Why *can't* you be confused? I know that *I* was." He tilted his head over her. "But now I also know that I want it all too, *cara.* I want to be both those things, *all* those things, for you." He released one of her wrists in order to lift his hand to her head and dig it against her scalp. He kept up the pressure, steadily pulling, letting her know the words weren't play for him. "Why can't we find both sides of ourselves, on this amazing journey, together?"

He yearned to bend down, closing the inches between them to kiss her. But her eyes swam in unsteady emerald pools, depths that looked so much like the emotional version of kerosene. Imagine *that.*

He forced himself to stop as she took in a shaky breath, preparing her next words.

"Because there can't be a journey."

Though she was still captive to his hold, she closed him out for a moment as if summoning supernatural help for her next words. When she reopened her eyes, the shadows in them had turned into chasms. She raised her hand to cover his. "I've accepted a transfer to the JAG Region Legal Service Office in Atsugi, Japan."

For a long second, it seemed she'd issued the words in another language. They were like gibberish, syllables he didn't expect.

"What?"

He loosened his hold and finally stepped back from her altogether. "*Japan?*"

"Yeah. I—I leave on January second."

"What. The—"

He grunted, unable to finish. All her cat-in-the-rain behavior now made a shitload more sense and twisted his gut in a thousand more ways.

She hadn't come here tonight for their new start. She'd come to say goodbye.

"I've been prepping a case in conjunction with their office," she explained. "The CO is short on advocates for his team, so—"

"So you just volunteered to move yourself six thousand miles. Is that it?"

A breath rushed out of her. It was edged with more tears. "Dante—"

"Wait. Let me correct that," he spat. "Six thousand miles away from *me*. That hits the mark a bit better, doesn't it, *cara?*"

She had the nerve to close the three steps between them again and grab his hand. "Listen to me. We're only flying this op at low altitudes right now, okay? We haven't gotten to the tough stuff yet."

"Because you're moving to *Japan*."

He wrenched free from her, stomped back to the bar, and

dumped more Scotch into a glass. The liquid never hit his lips. He glared down into the gold fluid, too shocked and enraged to even drink his way into a decent stupor.

A silent minute stretched into another. Another. Celina broke into the fourth one with a trembling voice.

"My brother Dylan flies F-18s for a living. They're fifty-million-dollar jets. But if the plane is headed for disaster, the navy doesn't expect the pilot to hang on and try to save the plane. They're ordered to eject their ass and get out safely." A sad huff escaped her. "We can't hang on to this op, Dante. The view looks great right now, but—"

"View?" He slung a bitter laugh. "You have no idea what you're talking about. There's no *view*, Celina. This flight has barely cleared the tower, and you're already grounding us."

"That's not true, damn it."

"No?" He wheeled, snapping his head toward her a second after his body led the way. She wet her lips and grabbed the couch for balance, confirming he'd accomplished the daunting purpose of the move. But he had no intent of stopping there.

"Are you telling me you didn't yearn for me to help you back out of that sweater Saturday night instead of into it? Are you standing there expecting me to believe you didn't want more, *stellina*? Much more? You want me to believe that you didn't want me to come back in as soon as I left? That you didn't long to go back into that playroom with me and have me strip you, bind you, mark you, fuck you?"

With each question, he took another pair of steps in a circuitous path around her, deliberately circling and watching, introducing new visuals into her head with his growling cadence and his blatant words. And it was working. He watched her chest pump faster beneath her sinful dress. He noticed her hands at her sides, curling with the effort to keep her composure in check.

When he stopped, he was just a foot away from her. He braced his feet and then folded his arms. "Yeah, I call bullshit on your defense, counselor. With every word of it. But I'm done trying to talk about it."

That caused a fast raise of her gaze. She couldn't hide the lingering sorrow in her face or the resigned jerks of her nod. "I understand."

Dante chuffed. "No. You don't." He moved his hands to his sides now. "I said I'm done talking about it. I said nothing about not proving it in other ways."

"Wh-What do you mean?"

Before he spoke again, he reached and unclasped the brooch at her waist. He tossed the jewelry to the coffee table. The action didn't make her dress fall open, but it sure as hell loosened everything up. He now peeked at a red demibra and matching red spaghetti panties. Fucking hell. If this didn't work, he'd be in a cold shower until midnight.

"You're going to Japan," he stated. "Fine. I can't stop that. But that means that *this* is what we have left. Now. Tonight. So, game on, *stellina*. You say you're fine with ejecting from the flight? Then let's make you're really goddamn sure about yourself."

Her breath hitched as he stepped closer, cranking the burners in his blood higher. He clutched a handful of her hair, this time with hot and determined intent, pulling her head back for his lunge of a kiss. He ended the assault by sliding his mouth down to the defiant crest of her chin and biting her there.

"You're going to go mach five with me tonight, Celina, or

you're going home. It's your choice. If you stay, we're going to the bedroom, and you *will* submit to me. Let me be clear about how this will go. You'll sob, you'll scream, you'll moan, and you *will* come, more than once. But first, you'll give me your body in any way I want, as many times as I want. If you want to go home now, then that's all right too. I wish you a wonderful adventure, Pippi Longstocking; send me a fucking postcard."

He released her as gently as he could, but he wasn't feeling magnanimous right now. His senses flailed in a tangle of frustration, fury, and the raw claw of lust. He wanted to punish her. He needed to fuck her. He longed to brand her, body and soul, in any way he could before she left his life. He wasn't about to tell her that GRI had expansive offices in Tokyo too, or that he enjoyed the use of a penthouse on top of them nearly as opulent as this. She'd made the decision to go because she needed space—six thousand miles of it—from him. It was done. He had no control over that part. But if she stayed now, it was time for him to take back a few bunkers in the camp known as Celina Kouris's mind. He was going to make damn sure that even six months and a fourteen-hour time difference didn't make him easy to forget.

"I'm going to the kitchen," he told her. "I need a drink of water, and you probably do too. When I get back, I want you either naked or gone."

His stride across the living room was wide because of the pounding crest in his jeans. He could've gotten the waters at the bar, but he had to get out of lunging distance from her. If he stayed near, she wouldn't have a choice about things. She'd be under him on the floor in two seconds and then spread for him in another two. He wanted to be many things for her, but an assaulting monster wasn't one of them.

That didn't mean he was going to be leisurely about this, damn it. He picked up his pace, punching on the kitchen lights and then ripping two glasses out of the cabinet. With a suppressed growl, he jammed them into the water dispenser. He'd never been more in a hurry in his life. He needed to know if hell was coming in twelve minutes or twelve hours.

CHAPTER FOURTEEN

Celina watched his shadow through the frosted glass between the living room and the kitchen. He moved like a man possessed, which meant she needed to stop standing here like a nimrod and move just as quickly. She needed to choose. Pick a path and commit.

Path? Oh, right. One of those. The two directions Dante had issued to her as an ultimatum, both *not* on her list for how this "chat" was supposed to shake out. Correction. She *had* planned for both options, just not getting them handed to her on a platter of seething fury, served with an entrée of scorching sexuality, a side of kiss-me-until-my-pussy-trembles, and a sauce on top of it all called mind-blowing Domination.

"What the hell are you doing, Cel?" Though she issued it under her breath, its wild desperation surrounded her. This was what she'd wanted, right? She'd picked this trip over an e-mail on the desperate hope he *would* take this to the bedroom, though as the conversation worsened, she'd bet closer to him dealing a cold *Don't let the door hit you on the way out.* She'd never expected his command for *her* to make the decision—especially with his personal "touches" on things.

If you stay, you will *submit to me. You'll sob, you'll scream, and you'll give me your body in any way I want, as many times as I want.*

"Shit," she whispered. "Shit, shit, shit!"

Could she do this? Just serve herself up on his sexual

platter like this? What she'd seen on Saturday, between Rose and Mark Moore—surely they'd worked their way up to being with each other like that, right? What Dante proposed for her tonight, the absolute authority that defined every step he now took back toward her, the hard purpose that redefined the jaw beneath his beard, was not "working up to things."

She was paralyzed as he approached. One half of her feared the hell out of him. The other half wanted him in more ways than she'd ever dreamed. He was truly a demon incarnate now, defined by utter darkness across his features and in his stride.

He slammed the drinks to the coffee table. "You're not gone."

She summoned her best obstinate courtroom face. Well, tried to. "N-No."

"And you're not naked."

"You didn't give me even a minute, Flash Gordon. This is a lot to process!"

"I know the fucking feeling."

He deliberately dug that one in with gritted teeth.

Celina coiled her arms across her chest. "Are we going to fight again? I'm trying here, Dante. I came here to—"

"To what?" He yanked her arms apart. "To do *what*, Lieutenant Kouris?" He flung the formality at her with even harsher emphasis. "What the hell do you want, Celina? I even gave you a choice. *What do you want?*"

Wind whipped at the glass windows behind him. Emotions blasted her with equal force. Fury. Desire. Sadness. Madness. A million more, whipping like papers in a hurricane. Those papers were hers, damn it, the tidy piles she'd filed perfectly in the drawers of her mind. Not anymore. Even after she landed in Tokyo, they wouldn't be righted for a very long time to come. That meant she had no directions. No idea what to think, what to say, what was wrong or right anymore. She squeezed her eyes shut, just wanting to slam the drawers closed and burn the papers. Just needing to succumb to one action, the only action that made sense right now.

She slowly opened her eyes. With equal deliberation, she looked past his rage-tight temples and ink-thick lashes, straight into the deep midnight of his glare. She stepped closer, moving to stand nearly hip to hip with him before pressing one hand over his chest.

"What do *you* want?"

Ten seconds of silence went by. Twenty. Celina didn't move her hand, which became the only way she knew he still breathed. His lips finally parted a little. His jaw rotated, a slow version of that hungry contemplation that never ceased to make her feel like the last bite of food left on earth.

"Ask me again," he directed quietly. "But address me as your Sir this time."

She took her own turn at the no-breathing thing. Her gaze dropped in time to watch her fingers tremble against his sternum. "What do you want...Sir?"

They sucked in air together. As Dante exhaled, he cupped the back of her head. "Damn it, *stellina.* That's more beautiful than I imagined it would be."

The praise filled her with joy. She burrowed against him, roping a hand around his neck, treasuring this moment of feeling their hearts throbbing together. Because her ear was pressed to his chest, she felt his resulting growl before it hit the air. When it did, he purposely scooted her away. It was like her action had rammed a button of deeper fury inside him.

With sharp tugs, he yanked free the tie on her wraparound. He opened his lips more, revealing his locked teeth as he pulled the dress apart and shoved it off her shoulders. A new wind gust hit the windows as the red fabric pooled at her feet.

Dante's breath rushed out of him with sensual force. "Fuck. Me."

Celina shifted from foot to foot. She'd blushed her way through purchasing the red lingerie set, having no idea there could be so many choices for shit that covered so little. Crazily, the least expensive part of the set was the most concealing. The red fishnets hit at the middle of her thighs and were attached to a matching garter belt that felt as awkward as doing the backstroke in a pair of kid's water wings.

"It's lame," she stammered. "Right? I had to put it all on by myself. I probably messed something—"

"Ssshhh." Dante waved a sharp hand. "It's not lame. Just let me look."

She bit her lip and stole a glance at him. Sure enough, he looked. And looked. And looked. His lips were slammed together now, working back and forth in an expression that bordered on a grimace. His nostrils flared in and out. And his stare... It was the most restless part of him, prowling up and down her body like a starving panther. The insane thing was, she actually felt like that animal under target. The sensation was incredible. She wondered if her jungle counterparts felt this too. The terror mixed with the anticipation, the pure fear of surrender, followed by the euphoria of being free. It made her dizzy. She actually swayed.

Shit. *Shit.* What was happening to her? Everything again rushed at her so fast, too fast. In an attempt at regaining control, she started babbling.

"I remembered how you liked the fishnets I wore on Saturday. Is red as good as the black? I didn't quite know if the fastenings—"

"*Stop.*"

The unfettered snarl of his voice was enough to enforce the order. In sheer shock and more than a little arousal, she obeyed. The monologue got shoved down her throat, and she fisted her hands at her sides. After that, she braced for the backlash from her brain, sure to hit any moment. Any second now, she was certain common sense would kick in and tell her how insane this was to be standing on display for her lover, waiting for him to issue another command at her.

That moment never came. Instead, everything kept careening forward, faster and harder than before. Every moment carried Dante forward too. The aura of his power flowed off him, weaving its way into the pores of his skin, the planes of his face, the sovereignty of his stance. He was mesmerizing.

She watched, not saying a word, as he came closer by a couple of wildcat-smooth steps. "Thank you," he said, making it sound more command than appreciation. "The fishnets are beautiful, but your silence pleases me even more. You had to think about it far more deeply than the stockings..." He reached down and unsnapped both her front garters. "Which are going to say their farewell now anyway."

He unhooked the back garters with both hands, letting his hands linger on the swells of her ass when he was done. Celina gasped as he palmed both cheeks and then gave them dual slaps, but a single word didn't fall from her mouth. As she breathed out the brief stings, hanging on to Dante's forearms for balance, a low hum emanated from him in return.

"Turn around," he instructed, physically guiding her in the action as well. "Hang on to the back of the couch, *cara*, and enjoy the view."

She wondered why there was a tantalizing edge to his tone—until she obeyed the order for the position and saw what he meant by "the view." Because the clouds outside were now thick as soup, the patio window had become a mirror. She lifted her head to see herself, bent over and waiting for whatever he wanted to do to her. Her breasts hung down, her nipples engorged with arousal, now barely tamed by the red bra. Her ass and her thighs were flares of flesh behind her.

Hell.

She needed to feel dirty about this. Wanton. Shameless. She needed to see herself being turned into his sexual play toy by increasingly bigger stages.

Yeah, she felt all those things.

And had never been more turned on in her entire life.

As if he read her mind, Dante moved up behind her, dark and graceful in his formfitting shirt and gray jeans. With slick surety, he slipped his hand between her thighs from behind. He didn't dip his fingers below her panties. He didn't have to.

"What's this I feel already, *stellina*? A sweet, wet pussy getting ready for me?"

She hissed and arched, her breath coming in shaky waves, but she didn't take her eyes off the figures in the window. She watched as if she were in an amazing erotic dream. If that was the case, she didn't want to wake up for a very long time.

Dante only made it better, lowering behind her and taking down both her stockings on his way. When he hit the tops of her boots, he unzipped those too and then lifted her feet one by one in silent instruction for her to step free. He tossed the shoes so they landed atop her dress on the floor. In the window, she could see him flow his stare over every inch of her again. She didn't blink or breathe as he slid a hand down to his crotch, palming the bulge there to greater hardness.

"Oh, *stellina*." He emitted a sound between a groan and a grunt. "You are one magnificent creature of torture."

Her vagina pulsed, sending another river into her panties. Driven by an unseen instinct, she staved off a shiver by starting to roll her hips. Even a sudden jarring comprehension didn't stop her.

Hell. Wasn't this exactly how things started the other night with Mark and Rose Moore?

"Holy shit," he said huskily. "Keep going, baby. You're so goddamn sexy, my beautiful *cara*."

She gave him a sighing cry. Her head swirled like the mist outside, flying into an atmosphere she'd never been in before. She extended her whimper, turning it into a sound of supplication as well as arousal. She wanted more, yearned to fly higher. Her whole body shook with need.

He shifted and pressed behind her again. His hand and fingernails formed a warm pressure down the length of her spine. "It's okay, baby. I'm going to give you everything you want, the same way you're going to give me everything I want. I promise it fully."

His words and his touch streaked fiery tingles through every inch of her skin. "Yes!" It left her lips before she could control it, which made the rest easier to spill. "Yes, Dante, please!"

He amped the fire by a thousand, cracking her ass with two more spanks. "Sorry, *cara*," he drawled. "Guess I wasn't clear enough the first time. Words aren't your duty right now, unless I demand them directly from you. And believe me, I *will* ask for them. But right now..." He closed his grip around her shoulders, bringing her back to her feet and holding her steady for a moment. "Let's take a little walk."

After her footing got steady, he took her hand and tugged her behind him down a mahogany wood hallway. The clean lines and modern angles reminded her of the hall they'd walked at Dark Escape, only here there were no sensual prints on the walls. Instead, there were several alcoves embedded with shelves that held a mishmash of photos. Every person in the pictures shared Dante's full mouth, strong nose, and longer-than-legal eyelashes. She almost felt the Tieri clan watching her walk behind their golden son, certain they all somehow knew exactly what he was about to do with her. And wishing they'd let her in on the secret.

At the end of the hall, he pushed open a set of double doors. He pulled her into a bedroom that surely had its own zip code. Celina supposed she should have guessed at the square footage just for kicks, but that option faded against the option of drowning a gasp of awe. It was a stunning room, with ivory carpet that cushioned her every step as she let him draw her closer to a four-poster bed with gauzy gold-flecked drapes that were suspended from the ceiling and flowed down each of the four corners, making decadent puddles when they hit the floor. Along the walls, artistic silhouettes of trees were backlit by deep-violet lighting, making the walls look like early twilight. Tall sleek urns overflowed with live plants, their earthy freshness mingling with Dante's signature patchouli to form an enchanted-forest bouquet.

She tilted her face up to him with a little smile.

Dante was already staring at her. Not smiling.

His look made her toes curl and the deepest parts of her sex vibrate. For some reason, she got even wetter as he released her hand and set her a few feet away from him. His pose rose by a few inches, nearly like a military commander setting straight a new recruit.

"Ground rules," he stated. "You already know the criterion for speaking, so I trust we don't have to review that. Your attire, for the moment, is"—he cracked a small smile—"ideal. But most importantly, let's talk limits."

In the pause he inserted, she lifted a confused look. Limits? Holy shit. Limits to what? She thought of the Moores again. Saturday night's "fun" had been in a high-end bondage club with huge equipment and trusses. Why did they need "limits" here in Dante's bedroom?

Again as if his brain had smart-synched to hers, Dante emphasized, "You get limits, *cara*, no matter where we are or how we play. We *always* go only as far as you say. You have words to use if you're too overwhelmed to go on. They even call them safe words. You say 'star' if you need everything to stop in full. You say 'sky' if you need to simply slow down. Got it?" He cut short the little nod with which she responded, directing her face to him with two fingers under her chin. "Why don't I believe you?"

She met his gaze directly. "That's a direct question, right?"

He sighed. "Yes, *cara*. And I want it answered."

"Are those words really necessary? Why don't I just tell you to stop?"

He stepped back again. "Because there's a good possibility you *will* use that one." A small smirk again tilted his lips. "But you'll be too hot and wet to *mean* it."

She could tell he expected a crack from her at that. She

didn't have one because her imagination proved him right. She saw herself on the bed beneath him, his hand smacking her backside and her fervent screams of "Stop!" filling the air. He was right. It pumped her sex full of heat.

"I've got a few surprises for you, *stellina*." Neither his face nor his voice lost their overlay of sensual knowingness. "Why don't you get up on the bed and make yourself my star there?" He used a hand at the side of her head to fix her gaze once more to his face and its darkening intent. "That means I want you on your hands and knees, head low, ass high. Are these instructions clear? You may answer 'Yes, Sir' or 'No, Sir.'"

The storm mist invaded her senses again. Hot and cold fronts slammed together in her body. She shouldn't love those words, and yet the harder edge to them sizzled to her sex like lightning bolts to a grounding point. "Yes," she answered, hating the breathy edge of it. "Yes, Sir, that's clear."

His touch tightened by a fraction. "That's my good girl."

Forget the lightning in her pussy. Her whole body became live electricity now, the excuse she used for walking to the bed on legs that wobbled like a baby's. She shook even worse as she got up on the plush cover and maneuvered herself into the position he'd dictated.

Head low. Ass high.

Oh *hell*.

The instructions, even issued from his incredible lips, had sounded like a first-class invitation into humiliation. But kneeling here with her body like this, in the middle of this luxurious bed and its shah's share of pillows, she felt like a jewel. No, wait. What was that word Mark Moore used on Rose? A pet. A gorgeous, loved pet, waiting for her Master to return and—

She swallowed hard as her mind filled in the rest of that thought.

She heard water splashing, some drawers sliding, and a closet door being slammed shut. Finally, Dante came back in with a purposeful stride. He'd taken his shirt off, which should have been an incredible distraction, but he took care of any appreciation she'd give his muscled torso with the kink arsenal he bore. The rolling waist-high rack riveted her stare and made her heart pump to the point of pain. Or maybe that was her body's way of telling her what was in store for her. Hanging from a vertical top bar, about two feet across, were a hanging collection of things she recognized, like wood paddles, leather floggers, a riding crop, and even something that looked like a feather duster, but it was the tiered shelf next to the hanging toys that dealt her the blow of fear. Ohhhh hell... So many of those things would never possibly fit inside her body. Their pretty turquoise glint didn't fool her, especially with the large tube of lubricant that sat next to them.

"*Stellina.*" Dante's tone was thick with reprimand. "I believe I said head low, not face tilted around and sneaking peeks?"

"Y-Yes, Sir." She snapped her head back down, though the mental explosion had already started. She'd already seen Dante begin to reach for the rack. Shit, shit, shit; what had she gotten herself into? *Safe words.* She had to remember she had those. Star and sky. But even those were teasing little things. They sounded more like a couple of new anime toys for Sami rather than words to make him stop with *his* toys. This was insane. What was she doing here, and why did it still make her deepest folds quiver with anticipation and tighten with need? And why oh why did she shiver all over, in all the best ways, when she felt one of his hands cupping her ass...and then slowly caress its way up her spine...and then run its way through her hair?

"Ssshhh," he murmured, now backtracking that hand. He pulled her hair out of the way with it. Only then did she realize she was breathing like a sprinter. "You need to trust me, *cara*. Take some deep breaths. Trust me."

"I—I do." She hoped her earnest tone told him how strongly she needed to say it. His deep hum conveyed his approval. She actually did begin to breathe easier...

Until he slipped something over the top of her head. Something with a tight band around it. Seconds later, the world went blacker than his eyes.

Oh God. A blindfold?

"Remember how you trust me?" His voice flowed around her as she felt him rustling toward the headboard, seeming to rearrange the pillows. Then his touch descended on her again, gentle yet firm, sliding down one arm. Celina almost reached up with her other hand to rip the eye covering away, but his fingers felt so good, so commanding, so encompassing as they circled the insides of her elbows and trailed like whispers to her wrist, right before he wrapped something around that too. The binding was soft and possessed the naughty scent of leather.

Leather.

Shit.

She jerked her arm, trying to move it. And got nowhere.

He'd tethered her to the bed.

By the time the conclusion hit her, Dante had already secured her other wrist.

"*Stellina,* you really need to breathe."

What did he *think* she was doing? Celina shot the silent retort between her lungs' effort for air. "I—" she managed out loud. "This—Dante, this is—"

The press of a strong hand came down to her head again. "Didn't you say you trust me?" His grip tightened, pulling at her scalp a little. "That was a direct question, *cara.*"

"Yes." She drew out the last of it in a fuming hiss. "Yes, I do trust you, but—"

"And didn't I tell you we were going to take this to mach five tonight?"

"In the first ten minutes?"

She tensed, half expecting him to direct some attention at her ass again because her inner smacktard couldn't keep a lid on it. Instead, she felt him dig his other hand into her hair and then pull hard enough that all the inner chitchat was silenced too.

"Celina, we haven't even taken off yet."

She said nothing to that and probably couldn't if she tried. She fought another rush of dizziness and then wondered why. Where was she going to fall? Onto this cloud of a bed? Oh damn it all if *that* happened. She was, whether she wanted to admit it or not, truly safe.

With the acceptance of that, her senses were suddenly free to recognize other things. She trembled and sighed as she did just that. The scrape of the bra as her nipples now pressed at the edge of it, pouting in hard arousal. The exposed line of her body, ready for any touch from him. And oh God, the kiss of her moist panties on her sensitive labia.

"All right, sweet girl. I'm going to ask nicely just once again. Do you trust me?"

His question came in a voice she'd never heard from him

before. He drew out each syllable like a caress, deliberately taking his time with them, the tone so different from his urgent commands during the other times they'd been together. There was a pressure beneath in these sounds too, but it lay tethered and coiled, waiting for its moment to strike, becoming a force all its own even through the darkness that defined her vision, perhaps because of it.

She couldn't see him, so she imagined him. He swirled to life in her mind as an even more magnificent satyr of sensuality. She saw his arms bunching as he pulled her hair, envisioned his sculpted bronze chest looming over her and his hair tumbling against his beard. He surrounded her with his touch, his presence, his hands, his focus. A rough rumble emanated from him as he moved onto the bed with her, his weight dipping the mattress behind her.

"I'm waiting, *stellina.*"

"Yes." It felt like a giant weight tumbling out of her mouth. He'd ordered her not to talk, but now it felt like dragging her tongue through mush to get simple words out. "Yes, Sir. I trust you."

Another growl, heavier and harder, vibrated from him. "My sweet *cara.* Do you know how much that pleases me? How beautiful it is, coming from your lips?" With a quiet slip of movement, he tucked two fingers beneath her panties from behind. "And apparently, you're ready to be pleasured as well."

She groaned as he instantly found the sweet spot of her clit. In tandem to her reaction, Dante delivered a sharp swat to her backside. The sound in her throat became a shriek at her lips—but it was a sound of surprise, of wonder, perhaps a little delight. The double whammy of sting and stimulation was incredible.

"Shit," she blurted before knowing she'd even done so. "Dante! Ohhh yes!"

His answering spank, now dealt to the opposite ass cheek, came with a grip on her pussy that punished this time. But the pinch of his fingers was a mild preamble to what came next.

"In the way," he said tightly before twisting his other hand into her thong. With one fierce jerk, he tore it away. She barely had time to gasp in surprise when she felt something like a small chain brushing her backside—just before something else, hard and tight, bit into one side of her labia. Before she could yelp at the shock of that, the same treatment was given the other side. The chains jingled against her ass cheeks as Dante extended them from between her legs, wrapping one around each thigh, before clasping them back on themselves. The chains hit her thighs where the fishnets had just been. The irony of the change didn't escape her. The stockings had helped land her here, where she wanted to be, but she hadn't fathomed it would be like this. She had no idea he was going to open her like this, plunging her eyes into darkness while his saw everything, exposing her to him in the most basic and primal way...

She had no idea it would spin her brain so far from her body.

"Damn it, Dante!" She clung to the words as much for sanity as a furious release.

"You mean damn it, *Sir*?"

"Fine. What the hell is this, *Sir*?"

The man actually chuckled. "A little reminder about controlling your verbosity, *stellina*. Marker Man told me how effective these little devices could be." To add insult to injury, he trailed a finger between her ass cheeks and then farther, gently stroking the tongue of her clit again, now totally exposed with her pussy lips stretched back. Her body sent back a wave of arousal, pounding more blood against the tight clamps. "What he didn't tell me was how perfect you'd look like this, with your gorgeous cunt clamped and your clit held hostage for me. You are perfect, my *stellina*."

She whimpered, digging her head into the bed, not wanting to enjoy this humiliation at all. But God help her, she did. The constricting pain went to battle with his merciless strokes, turning her pussy into a wild mess of resistance and then need, every second sending a new impulse to her brain. Like she could even form a coherent thought now. She was conscious of her hips rolling and bucking, alternately fighting him and needing him. Dante's gruff breaths were a visceral goad, especially because she could focus so clearly on them. She nearly felt them vibrate through him as he started to meet her thrusts with both his hands, delivering little slaps and finger scrapes to her hot, tingling skin.

Soon his smacks turned into spanks. The scratches turned into tougher rubs. Celina gyrated harder into his rhythm. The clamp chains jingled on her thighs. Her mind whirled even more like the wind outside, yet a tiny part of it still screamed at her. It bellowed that Celina Kouris didn't do things like this. Celina Kouris didn't bump and grind to the point that bondage chains banged against her thighs. Celina Kouris didn't moan in delight from behind a blindfold as her lover murmured what a good girl she was and how hard she was making his cock.

Screw Celina Kouris.

For now, for tonight, for just these few beautiful hours, she just wanted to be *stellina*.

"*Stellina?*"

"Yes," she sighed. "Yes, Sir."

"Are you still with me?"

How did he know? The question filled her with more awe for him. How did he know to ask that as if he knew exactly where her mind was, flying higher by the minute, lost to this ether where thought evaporated and she was just a ball of raw sensation? She decided she didn't care. She was only grateful. Deeply, profoundly grateful.

"I—I think," she managed to stammer.

"Good," he said. "Very good, *bellissima. Lei è la mia buona ragazza. Merda, vorrei montarti.* I'm so damn hard, looking at you like this."

Between the fuzz in her ears and the heat through her body, she had an even worse time trying to pick through the music of his foreign words. It didn't matter. His graveled tone spoke his meaning clear enough. Whatever he wanted to do to her, she was more than ready.

Except what he did next.

"Time to come down for a little bit, baby. Take a deep breath."

He waited just three seconds more before reaching and freeing the pussy clamps.

"*Dante!*"

Her rushing blood hit in an agonizing rush, making her pull against the cuffs. She clenched her thighs and writhed, thinking surely things would get back to normal down there in a second. No such luck, damn it.

"Keep breathing, *cara.* You're doing so well. It'll feel so much better in a minute, I promise." He leaned over her, swiping one hand across her ass and the other up and down her back.

A minute? He wanted her to wait a whole minute? "I—I can't!"

"Ssshhh. Breathe through it."

"Shut. Up."

The words were barely out when the hand at her ass lifted, coming down in a pair of fast whacks. "I said I'll give you what you need, Celina. When did you stop believing that?"

She let him have only a seething moan. But somewhere between the start and the end of that sound, something amazing happened. A new sensation flooded her sex. Warmth. No, heat. A rushing, enveloping, better-than-a-vibrator jolt of it. All the blood the clamps had staved off now had a massive reunion party with her labia, her clit, even her inner thighs. It was such a shock, she forgot to be mad anymore, even when Dante's low chuckle filled the air from above.

"Do you trust me now, *stellina*? And yes, you can certainly answer that."

"Y-Yes. Okay. All right. I trust you, Sir. I do. Oh shit!" She cried it out when the press of his hand came again, tracing a confident path through her wet folds before he deepened the probe into her convulsing core. First one finger twisted at her pussy. Then two. His thrusts filled the air between them with a moist, rhythmic music.

"And do you believe now that a few nips of pain can turn into a great deal of pleasure?"

She scowled, not caring if he saw. It hadn't been just a "few nips." Wisely, she held that back. But she couldn't fling a single word of argument about the pleasure. Waves of the stuff hit her even now, like a rising tide against the shore, surging, sensual, uncontrollable. As Dante worked a third finger into her vagina, her senses lifted off from that beach and into the clouds once more. Ironically, she felt her head fall as the sensation took over.

"Celina? An answer?"

"All right!" she retorted. "Yes; yes, you're right. Pain...can lead to pleasure..."

"Good girl. Whose pleasure?"

She squirmed. "I can't just say that!"

He withdrew his index finger and joined it with his thumb to form a new clamp on her labia. The skin was still sensitive, and she winced.

"*Whose pleasure*, Celina?"

"Wh-Why the hell are you forcing this?"

"To make you hear how beautiful you are." His voice was rough as his touch. "And to make you remember it, for a very long while to come. To make sure you remember me." He twisted his grip on her aching tissues before commanding again, "Whose pleasure, Celina?"

"Damn it! M-Mine!"

It felt like nails on a mental chalkboard to talk about herself like this, but partly because his fingers wouldn't accept anything else from her. But oh God, pleasure was just the beginning of what his touch fast turned into, now softening into a glorious massage on her folds. He shifted a little again until his fingers stroked her clit and his thumb arched up to prod the ring of her ass.

She gasped. She'd never been touched there before, and his naughty little circles around the sensitive rim were like a taste of the most forbidden nectar on earth. "Ohhhh!"

His low, confident hum warmed the air. "Now admit I was right."

"Right...about what?" To be honest, he could've directed her to agree they'd get a heat wave tomorrow, and she'd acquiesce. Not that she'd say so out loud.

"I promised you'd get what you need." He rolled his touch, his fingers incessant at both her clit and her anus. "Are you getting what you need, *cara*?"

"Ohhh shit!"

He gave her thigh a sharp swat. "My answer?"

She glowered. This time, she hoped he saw it. The man was becoming very fond of spanking her.

"Yes," she snapped. "You know that's true, so why do you—*owwww*!"

He gave her another smack. This one smarted. He dealt it to the exact same place as its predecessor, burning the skin atop her hip bone.

"Why don't you rephrase that statement, counselor?"

She could tell he smirked his way through that order. Celina's stomach knotted in preparation for the backlash her mind was about to deal. *Counselor.* Why did he have to go there? But why *wouldn't* he go there? He probably thought it was a compliment. No, *no.* Dante had seen places inside her from the start, places she often didn't see herself. Tonight of all nights, he had to realize how she'd fought so many parts of herself, especially that methodical lawyer, just to walk into his building. So he had to know. He had to realize that any minute now, that word would yank her out of this sensual bliss and into the world where she remembered exactly who she was and why she shouldn't be doing this with him.

Anguish tore at her heart and stung her eyes. *Damn it!* She routed through her mind for his silly safe word.

Her mind.

Wait. Her mind. It was all still here. Of course it was. *She* was all still here.

She shook her head, feeling blinded even in this darkness. She hadn't left Celina Kouris behind at all. Celina had been right here. Not forgotten, simply changed. Opened. Awakened. And damn him, *bless* him, Dante knew that too. She could still be every inch the counselor in choosing to be submissive. When her body knelt for him, her spirit had never stood taller. And in the surrender she gave to him, she'd never given more power back to herself.

The light of the revelation intensified. It suddenly all made sense, a prism of breathtaking logic, a gift from this act she'd looked at as the most insane thing she'd ever done in her life.

Wanting this, craving this, wasn't some dirty secret hidden in her psyche. It spoke to the very heart of who she was. Just like the man who'd given it to her. The person who'd burst into her world with larger-than-life force had also given her a larger-than-life lesson.

In return, he only asked one thing. Her submission. He didn't even demand forever. He was willing to take just this tiny bubble of time, a dark and beautiful escape of their own, where they discovered these amazing parts of themselves together.

And right now, she wanted exactly the same thing.

CHAPTER FIFTEEN

Dante knew he'd hit a nerve with the word. It was the precise reason he'd used it.

It was a ballsy gamble, reminding her of everything she'd had to shove away just to walk in here tonight. But fuck it, he didn't want just slices of her. Even now, he wasn't going to settle for that. From the second he'd laid eyes on her, he'd dreamed of uncovering every speck of her, an exigency that only began with her body. But he'd also counted on having months to do that, indulging in gentle peel-backs of her layers, one careful section at a time.

Gentle had to go out the window tonight.

So here he was, taking a chance on the emotional Russian roulette. He knew the possible consequences. He knew that any second, she'd slice the air with her safe word. Despite the drawl with which he'd spun his challenge, his gut braced itself to free her from the cuffs and walk her out the door.

Instead, as she'd done so many times since the moment they'd met, she stunned his soul—which carried instant ramifications in his cock.

She dropped her head again. This time, the movement was slow, sure, and very much on purpose. And holy fuck, she didn't stop there. The lower her face dipped, the farther she extended her arms, stretching them toward the bedposts until they disappeared into the decorative pillows, flat against the bed. She laid her head down next, though she turned her head so he could see the sweet, peaceful smile that pulled at her lips.

"I'm getting everything I need, Sir Tieri. Thank you."

If her gorgeous velvet tone didn't turn him inside out, then the way she raised her back end higher at him, offering it with crystal-clear suggestion, officially did. "But are *you* getting the same? What do *you* need?"

First, he had to keep himself from swallowing his tongue. Assuring it was in the right place, he returned, "Celina, if you really knew the answer to that..."

"Enlighten me." She rubbed her torso against the blanket and then added fast, "Please, Sir. I do want to know."

He indulged the temptation to swat her. "Speaking out of turn again, *cara*? Tsk-tsk, baby." This time he kept his touch on her skin, stroking the blooms of heat across her high, tight swells. The light toffee of her skin had started to pinken. Knowing he was the one who'd put that blush there... Christ, it was a turn-on like he'd never known. Even his balls throbbed now, demanding to be let out of their denim prison. Soon, damn it. God, he hoped, *soon*.

But not too soon. Right now, he planned to draw this all out as long as he could. To thoroughly enjoy the breathtaking fantasy who'd come to life in his bed. Yeah, the same one who now lifted a taunting pout at him from beneath her mask.

He almost laughed at this streak of cheek that had taken over his serious, steadfast Celina, but another action felt more right. Moving so he stood at the side of the bed again, he reached and ripped her mask off. As he expected, the action caused her to jolt and blink. But the second her gaze found his, she gave back as good a shock as he'd given. Her emerald eyes were filled with a mixture of things that stole his breath. Total desire. Total adoration. Total trust. All directed at him. All *for* him.

Holy fuck. What had happened to her in the darkness behind that mask? He looked down at the blindfold as if it would reveal its magic secret to him.

"Didn't you say we were only taking off?"

He tilted his head. Oh yeah, something had definitely happened inside that gorgeous head of hers. She'd spiraled fast toward the submissive high; that much was so plain, she should've just sprouted wings and flown around the room. But this development was different. This was a deeper barrier through which she'd pushed, a mental barricade she'd pulverized. And he was *not* complaining. Not one damn bit.

Not that he was about to let *her* know.

"And didn't I say your words were only for direct responses to questions?" He backed up the response with the single step he took back, letting her watch as he traced fingers over all the hanging implements he'd selected with her beautiful backside in mind. When he heard her breath snag as he arrived at a long, shiny black paddle, he smiled and pulled it free. *Perfect.*

"Now you'll use your mouth for something a little more useful, *cara*," he said as he stroked her cheeks with the polished wood. He finally rested the end of the paddle on her lips. "Kiss it." As he watched her obey, pressing her lips lightly to the wood, he hissed from the agony of the fantasy filling his mind. He longed for her to render the same service to his cockhead. "Lovely. So lovely, baby. Now do it again. Close your eyes this time and think of me taking that wood to your ass."

Shit. Just shit. She not only followed the directions to the letter but committed herself so fully to the act that he watched her thick lashes quiver against her cheeks and heard a low whimper in her throat. She was completely wrapped in what looked like arousal or fear, or perhaps a mind-fucking combination of the two. All he knew for sure was his own torturous mixture of impulses. Let her keep worshiping the damn paddle, giving him the most exquisite sight he'd had in thirty years of sexual experience, or man the hell up and get on with using the thing to brand her with his domination?

"Enough." His command was a coarse grate as he pulled the wood from her mouth, trailed it down the smooth plane of her back and then up over the rise of her backside, where the blush from his other swats already began to fade. Well, that wouldn't do.

"You need to be marked, *stellina.*" He dragged his fingers over the firm swells, coaxing her body into a higher arch for him. As he slid onto the bed again and moved behind her, he reveled in how the new position also gave him a stunning view of her pussy. The curls were moist, the folds red and plump. "Fuck, yes. You need to be marked by me."

He replaced his hands with the top of the paddle now, savoring the way her eyes drifted shut while he traced circles on her skin with the flat of the wood. After a minute of that, he dealt some careful, light taps on the meat of her buttocks. She tensed. He wiped his palm across the light marks he'd left.

"Warm already," he murmured. "Do you feel it, baby?"

She nodded. He didn't push her for anything more of a response. This time, he wanted her mind to slip and her senses to soar. The higher he could rocket her, the better, though he wasn't going to make the trip easy. He loved watching her shiver, sigh, pant, and writhe for him. They were all such incongruities to the persona she gave the rest of the world. They were all precious gifts to him.

He gave her another easy warm-up. Soon, she was rolling her hips and ass at him. Her shoulders bunched as she pulled at the restraints. He watched everything closely. The pace of her breathing. The dew of her perspiration. The tension of her neck. The pats didn't look like much, but he knew damn well what he was asking her to take, even now. Though the paddle was barely wider than a paint stir stick, he knew what it felt like. He'd tried every implement on that rack out on his own forearm first. Of course, he thought the preparation would help him draw out his self-control, should this exact dream ever truly come true. He couldn't have been more wrong on *that* particular note. He wondered if his dick would ever speak to him again after its enslavement in his pants for so long.

"Let's heat it up a little more, baby."

He got bolder with the smacks. Celina didn't say anything, but he saw the pillows rise as she gripped the wrist cuffs harder. Holy fuck, how he wanted to say something himself. The need burned to tell her what a dream come true she was, how every erotic script he'd written for the two of them could be burned in comparison to the reality, how deeply she moved him with this offering of herself. But wherever her head was, he wanted it there. It was time to lay down the first of the tougher strokes.

"Ohhhhh!"

Okay, she didn't scream it. But the sound wasn't a tra-la-la of joy. Dante gave her a few seconds to acclimate before dealing one more *thwack*, higher and harder than the first. This time as she groaned, he used his other hand to rub the marks and distribute the pain. He was damn glad he'd listened to every word of Mark's spanking tutorial.

"You're getting so hot now. Oh *cara, sei incredibile.* You have no idea what this is doing to my cock. And I'm going to make your little ass even hotter before we're through."

He didn't let her finish her responding mewl. He launched

into three strokes this time, dealt in different places along her ass and thighs. When he was done, three beautiful, deep-red lines went dark against the copper of her skin. "Beautiful," he murmured. "So goddamn beautiful."

She trembled and then turned her head against the mattress. Now he could see her face in profile. He froze for a second. The shiny tracks of her tears almost had him hurling away the paddle, but then he caught the little lift at the corner of her mouth. Comprehension hit him like an eight-wheeler. Though she was scared to death, she needed this as badly as he did—*all* of this, even the way he struck her hard enough to stain her skin. He recalled Mark's attempt at an explanation of this, how submissives with the tightest reins over their public selves were often the ones who fell hardest once the restraints were on. Catharsis, he'd said. Freedom, he'd explained. Needs unfulfilled by anything else in their lives. It had been all Dante could do not to roll his eyes at his friend, but now he silently apologized to the guy for his skepticism. The woman in front of him was living proof that the magic worked both ways, that Dominant and submissive absolutely could serve and sate each other.

The realization filled him with a giddy fullness and a wild freedom of his own. Despite his stalker-style craziness and then the stunt at Dark Escape, he'd actually reined himself back through all this. He'd grappled against the dread of scaring her with the Dom he really wanted to set loose. Not anymore. He unfurled that version of himself on a test run through the next half dozen smacks he issued to her, increasing the strength of each spank as he went. By the time he got done, they both panted hard for air. Celina's high-pitched cries tangled with his guttural grunts.

It was time for his senses to embark on a flight of their own.

The feeling was euphoric. At last, his logic detached from his body and left behind only the raw need to take, dominate, possess, and burn. Oh fuck yes, to burn...

He followed that instinct by reaching for one of the shelves on the toy rack. It didn't escape him that the move was tracked by his subbie's huge gaze, which bulged even bigger when he selected two specific items. He cocked his head and tilted her an encouraging grin, but her features barely moved. She blinked at him and then swallowed hard.

"*Stellina.*" He said it in a chiding tease. "I said I was going to make it hotter, didn't I?" Riding his new surge of boldness, he brought his open palm down on her backside. "And your answer to that is..."

"Yes." She made an attempt to give the word sweetly. An *attempt.* The trepidation lacing each of her words couldn't be missed. "Yes, Sir, that's what you said."

"*Sì.*" The little bite of fear in her voice temporarily took away his aptitude for English. "*Sì, sì. Ciò è buono, il mio piccolo cara...*"

As the praise spilled from his lips, the lube drizzled out of the tube. He kept pouring out the glistening gel, making sure it coated every inch of the tapered anal plug in his other hand. After he had the toy generously slicked, he positioned himself so his chest pressed along her back and his mouth nestled against her ear. With one finger, just as he'd done before, he began to steadily trace the rim of her anus.

"You asked about what I need, *bellissima.* Here is your answer. I need all of this, every minute of it, with you. *Only* with you. And I need to know I've claimed a place in your body nobody else has been before." He took a few seconds to bask in the joyous heat of her little back hole, clutching his finger as he pushed in deeper. "Have you been touched here before, baby? Give me honesty. I'll know it if you don't."

"No, Sir." It was the answer he expected and the rasping offering for which he'd hoped.

"No man's fingers in your delectable little asshole? No man's cock?"

"No! Never!"

He gave a rumble of approval, twisting his finger to get it deeper into her steaming tightness. "I wish I could stuff my stalk into your backside tonight, *cara.* But no—sshhh—" He tried to laugh off how much her nerves turned him way the fuck on. "I'm already bulging with too much need for your pussy, and you're already so primed for this..."

As he'd talked, he'd withdrawn his finger. As he finished, he pressed the plug into her.

"Damn!" she shrieked.

"Damn," Dante whispered. He turned his head so he could watch the turquoise silicone disappear into her body. He let his body follow suit as he trailed wet kisses down her spine, continuing to hold it there. She tried to shove the plug back out, but he reprimanded her with a trio of sharp spanks, which did their duty in making her go slack.

"*Rilassati, mio dolce.* Relax. The pain will go away. I promise."

He started moving the plug in and out of her body, fascinated and inebriated with the power of taking her like this. He added more lube to aid his invasion, but that wasn't such a wise move. With the added sex gel, his thrusts now had a beautiful wet soundtrack to accompany them. When Celina added her tentative aroused moans to that, the universe grabbed his cock and burned three words into it.

Fuck. Her. Now.

With a fevered swoop, he swung around and slid himself between her thighs. As he secured the plug deep in her ass again, gazing over her spread and ready for him, he shook his head in wonderment. *Merda,* how had he gotten so lucky? He thought of all the great masterpieces he'd seen in his life, of how he could gorge his eyes for *another* lifetime on all the Michelangelo, Donatello, Brunelleschi, and Botticelli he wanted, and still not behold anything as cathedral-worthy as this woman, so sweet and ready to serve him. Her willingness moved him. Her trust humbled him. Her beauty devoured him.

His arms coiled as he gripped both her thighs and opened her a little wider. He didn't have to test her body's readiness. He saw it. Her red and bruised ass quivered with anticipation. Her cunt lips gleamed with her juices as they grabbed at the air, pleading for his cock to breach them. And he so couldn't wait to accommodate that need.

"This is the part where we burn it into cinders, *stellina.* Are you ready?"

"Yes." It was more a sob than a word. Her follow-up was a collection of desperate rasps. "Yes, Sir! Please!"

As she issued the plea, he frantically shoved down his zipper, finally freeing his iron-hard staff. He could practically see the blood pulsing in the veins that stood out against his stretched skin. The broad purple head was soaked with pre-come. Thank fuck he'd slipped a condom into his pocket, though getting the damn thing on was an exercise in torture. Christ, even the brush of his fingertips at his balls made him hiss, as he fought the flood that slammed at his body's dam.

In a matter of seconds, he fitted himself against her. He gave the anal plug another decisive twist and then prodded the entrance of her tunnel with his white-hot tip. Beneath him, Celina let out a long, needy moan. Her shoulder muscles were an incredible landscape as she curled her hands around the edges of the cuffs. She bucked her hips, trying to slide her body back deeper onto his cock. He nipped that rebellion in the bud, digging his fingers hard into the front of her hips.

"No," he ordered. "If I only get this tonight, then I get all of it. Complete surrender, Celina. Everything. Now. Your body. Your mind. Your arousal. Your orgasm. You're going to give them all to me, sweet girl. Empty yourself into me."

I sure as hell plan on returning the favor.

She let out a high, shaking sigh. "I—I'll try. I will."

"Good." As he slid in by another inch, he angled his body over hers, digging his knees into the mattress and one hand into her hair. "You're my good girl. *Bellissima mio. Vorrei penetrarla.* I'm going to fuck you now, hard and deep. Goddamn, what you do to me..."

Before the words were finished on his lips, his penis was sucked in, gripped, and engulfed by her body. Celina's groan twined with his, though he was barely conscious of anything beyond his roaring blood, his hammering heartbeat. Her obedience was perfect. Better than perfect. He not only felt her submission in her soft and yielding muscles but in the very air between them, an electricity she openly channeled to him. He grabbed the gift and felt like fucking Thor with a thunderbolt in his hand. The bolt zapped through him, taking hold of him, pumping his hips faster, and twisting his grip tighter. Her head arched back as his fingers clawed her scalp. Skin slapped skin as he claimed her pussy with his cock.

"Take it," he ordered from locked teeth. "Take me. All of me."

"Yes!" Tears coursed down her face, running over her smiling lips. "Thank you, Sir!"

He used his grip on her hair to angle her head to the side. He dipped his own head to suckle the tears off her cheeks. "You're wet everywhere, aren't you?"

"Y-Yes, Sir."

"You love this, don't you, *stellina*?"

"Yes." She gasped as he rolled his hips, changing up the pressure so her G-spot got a nice visit from his cockhead. "Oh God, yes!"

"Your cunt is crying all over my *cazzo*, baby. I think it wants to come."

"Please," she answered. "Oh please!"

Her words hit him straight in the cock this time. But he was torn. He didn't want this to end. He gritted against the heat that beat inside his balls, taking one more moment to kiss the salty sweetness of her face again. "Please...what?"

She hiccupped, trying not to sob again and failing. "Please, Sir, I want to come."

"Ah, sì," he uttered. "Then you shall." The last threads of control snapped in his own body. Blinding fire erupted up his shaft. "Come for me, *cara*. Come with me. Fuck, *yes!*"

She shuddered and trembled. Her vagina clenched. A scream of pure passion spilled off her lips.

And he was gone.

His flood didn't stop, pouring from him in consuming, mind-robbing waves, tearing away all coherence. He felt his eyes roll back in his head as his cock now swam in a condom full of his seed, but the climax itself didn't let up. He was drained, consumed, and still her body mercilessly milked him. Was this what heaven felt like? Or...hell? At the moment, he didn't care. Angel or demon, the woman who writhed beneath him, still panting and sobbing in the grip of her own explosion, was well worth the price of his soul.

CHAPTER SIXTEEN

Celina tugged back the cuff of her coat, exposing the scuffed skin of her wrist. She ran fingers along the strip and picked up on the faint smell of the eucalyptus gel Dante had worked into her skin after setting her free from the cuffs. She closed her eyes, trying to commit the scent to memory.

Then wished, for a desperate moment, the marks could be tattoos instead.

The elevator's chime broke into her reverie. Both she and Dante looked up in curiosity. It was four a.m., and clearly he didn't expect anyone in here any more than she did. A building housekeeper with an apple doll face got on and nodded to him. She peeked at Celina with open curiosity.

"Good morning, Mr. Tieri."

"Good morning to you as well, Olga. Happy Thanksgiving."

"You too, Mr. Tieri." She glanced at Celina again. "You no go to work today, do you?"

"No, sweetie. Not today. Spending time with family, after I"—his face tightened—"see my friend off. You have a nice day, now."

"Yes indeed, Mr. Tieri. The turkey you give us is stuffed and ready!"

"I'm glad." His broad smile clearly charmed the woman down to her underwear. Celina wondered if Olga could see the sadness hiding behind it, hiding in the darkest parts of his eyes and holding back the edges of his lips. If she did, she didn't indicate it. She got off at the next floor, trundling her cleaning cart behind her.

When the doors closed, he didn't waste a second to turn on her. His smile was gone. Darkness ruled his gaze again. He stepped closer, backing her into the corner, but that didn't stop his advance. Before she could breathe, he sealed his lips over hers and then parted her with brazen intent. His tongue was rough, possessive, unrelenting. In short, it was pure completion.

The horrific sting began again at the backs of her eyes. Shit. *Shit.* She thought every tear in her body had surely washed down the drain during her epic-length visit to his shower. She was so wrong. This goodbye was going to be worse than she'd thought.

The elevator got to the ground floor. Before the doors opened, he jabbed on the 45 button, sending them back up.

"Dante—"

"Don't leave." He leaned and started suckling her neck. "Come back to bed with me. It's warm. You love my sheets. You love me on them."

"Damn it," she retorted. If he added any mention of his towel heater or his back-massaging abilities, she was toast. "You really didn't become CEO on your looks, did you?"

"No, ma'am." He shifted his mouth to the other side of her neck, pressing his advantage by fitting the ridge in his crotch to her now aching mound. Since he'd torn the covering for that area right off her body, she was bare beneath her dress, and they both knew it. "Stay with me a few hours more, *stellina.*"

He wouldn't beg her, something else they both knew. Aside from the Roman blood that filled his veins, he was a man hardwired for command—a third thing they both knew, a fact she'd never refute after last night.

She yearned to know so much more about him.

Which was why she had to let him go.

An image rooted in her mind, of her actually daring to bring Dante to Dad's for Thanksgiving dinner. Even though they were one brother down, he'd be skewered alive. Dylan and Nik would gladly take up the slack for Cameron in snarky blows and dirty looks. She could hear them now, tearing apart everything from his designer shoes on up to the product on his forty-three-year-old hair. After Dante decided he'd had enough, *she'd* be flayed and gutted too. The crappy thing was, she'd even deserve part of it. Okay, all of it. She'd have to stand and plead guilty to the crime of letting Dante touch her, more than once. Then admit that she liked it. Then own up that she'd probably let him do it again.

If that wasn't enough, she'd have to confront the hardest truth of them all. Not just to Dyl and Nik, but to herself. She'd have to accept the revelation that kept surging from the depths of her soul, refusing to be silenced—the realization that she'd slept with the enemy, with full intent and purpose this time, and now knew he wasn't such an enemy after all. The "carpetbagger asshole" had indeed come bearing a carpet—but it didn't hide dirty money. It held pure magic. And the ride he'd given was a journey she'd treasure forever.

No. *No.* The decision powered her enough to slip from beneath him and push the button for the lobby again. Carpet rides weren't for forever. That's why they were magic. They weren't real. It was time to get out of here and put her feet on the ground again. It was Thanksgiving. She had things to do, including a lot of packing. Thirty-seven more days was going to pass very quickly.

She hoped.

After he bit out a string of Italian she did *not* want translated, Dante followed her into the lobby and out to the porte cochere. The Jag was waiting, already started up and idling, likely to warm up the interior. Vincent stood across the driveway, huddled against the freezing air and grabbing a cigarette. He gave them both a nod as they came out and then took the tactful approach and decided his cig was suddenly very interesting. Nevertheless, Dante pulled her farther away, out onto the sidewalk where the building's lights didn't reach.

In the shadows, with his determined stare fixed to her, he instantly turned back into the Dom who'd given her the best night of ecstasy in her life. Okay, that was an ideal explanation. She tried to hang on to that. Focusing purely on what they'd given each other's bodies was the perfect way to get through this. She used that to encourage a saucy little grin to her lips, and she glanced up him from beneath her lashes.

"Well, Mr. Tieri. Thank you. I hope it was as good for you as it was—"

"Shut up, Celina."

He curved a finger under her chin and forced her gaze up. His touch was like the handle of a furnace, even though he wore nothing but his sweats and a black crew sweater. But his face was the fire that decimated her. His eyes, twin coals of intensity, added to the heat from his hand, branding her to the bone. His forehead creased and his lips parted, making his features a portrait of raw torment.

Her breath clutched. She curled one hand into his sweater and the other into his beard. As her senses got lost in the dark-indigo fires in his gaze, she silently pleaded for his kiss. Just one more. Just one more whirl on the magic carpet before she reclaimed her life, her control, and her sanity, if that were possible. In so many ways, she wished it wasn't.

He leaned closer. The cloud of his breath mingled with hers.

He didn't kiss her.

"You remember when you ordered me to stop with the *stellina* shit?" He shook his head, chuffing softly. "Too late. You know why?" He pressed his hand over hers, in the center of his chest. "The earth moves. The moon does too. The constellations change. But the stars are still there. And you, Celina Kouris, are always going to be right here. You can't change that, even six thousand miles away, *mia stellina di prodigio.*" One side of his mouth lifted as tiny snowflakes dotted the air around them. "You're always inside me, my star of wonder."

★ ★ ★

The timing on this heartache crap couldn't suck more.

She tried the old-fashioned American approach of dousing the emptiness in every holiday tradition she loved and even a few she'd never tried before. Shopping. Lights. Eggnog. Lights. Wreath-making class. Lights. No matter what she tried, getting her yule groove on was not turning the Dante switch off.

It didn't help that he was everywhere.

The Daley Plaza Christmas Tree ceremony? Sponsored by GRI.

Some Central Shelter pups needing homes for Christmas? He plucked up the first one.

Needy kids getting their own free-play hours at the Navy Pier Wonderfest? Another GRI sponsorship.

Maybe the man was trying to drown his own misery in the merry-merry.

The thought made her heart clutch. And her head really pissed off.

What the hell are you doing? Just tune him out. Shut him off.

Ha. Easier said than done, especially because every ho-ho-ho action the man took brought a flurry of local press love— and the inevitable incredible pictures too. Hating herself for every second, Celina pored over each photo like the sick stalker she'd once accused him of being. When she was sure nobody was looking, she'd run a tender finger over the handsome face in the society pages—only to frown when she looked deeper at the images. His shoulders were too stiff. His smile was more porous than newsprint. Didn't anyone else see all this? Was anyone there to get angry at how tired he looked, to order him to slow the hell down and lighten the hell up?

The only picture that gave her hope was the shot of him and his new puppy. The shot, taken on that incredible couch of his, showed him next to a Christmas tree that looked plucked out of a State Street window. The pooch was a swoon-worthy yellow Lab. He looked happy and satisfied, like he'd finally decided to get on with his life too.

That was before she found out what he'd named the puppy. Star.

Celina had tossed that article into the trash can and then taken the rest of the afternoon off, claiming she needed to get in some packing. She put up eight more packages worth of lights on the house and then sat on the front lawn and watched the star-shaped bulbs glowing in the twilight. It wasn't long before the lanterns turned into golden blobs instead. Eyes brimming with tears did that to one's vision.

"Idiot," she muttered at herself. *You want him. He wants you. There are twenty more days until you leave. What's the harm of taking one more magic carpet ride? How much worse can the crash landing be than this?*

"Worse," she commanded back. "Don't do it, Cel. Don't do it. Just get this part the hell over with. Just a few more days, and it'll be better."

Dear God, it had to get better.

She still caved to a moment of weakness the next day. After sneaking out of the office "for some air," she pulled out her cell and punched in his direct office number. But before the line could click through, big brother came to the rescue in the nick of time. Dylan was calling from the base; he'd been called up on one of his famous last-minute, it's-a-favor-for-the-CO flights, and would Celina like some one-on-one time with her niece before shipping out for the Land of the Rising Sun? Thinking three days with an eleven-year-old wild child was just the distraction she needed, she picked Sami up from school and dragged her promptly to the grocery store for supplies to bake *Kourambiedes*. Despite Sami's horrified glance, she'd persisted. How hard could coated butterball cookies be, right?

She had, of course, burned the whole first batch. Sami sheepishly suggested the web site for *Good Day Chicago*. Some really cool guy was on it just this morning, she explained, detailing the finer points of *Kourambiedes* creation. They'd yanked up the site on her laptop.

That "really cool guy" was Dante. Who, in the course of the segment, was more than happy to tell the show hostess how passionate he'd suddenly gotten about Greek food. The perky blonde flashed a flirtatious smirk and joked about researching her family tree for some hidden Greek DNA.

Celina had slammed the laptop shut, ditched the cookies, and bought ten more boxes of lights.

By the time Christmas Eve came, Dad had decided that since her place was now the official beacon into outer space for any aliens seeking a holly-jolly rager, the family's holiday festivities for this year would be relocated to her living room. He gave her all of twelve hours' notice for the switch, however, meaning that when she opened the door for him on the twenty-fourth, she'd just gotten done setting the world's record for the fastest tree-trimming job.

After he greeted her with a bone-crushing hug and a buss to her forehead, Dad turned his piercing green stare onto her drooping tree. "Well." He sighed. "At least you got it up, *paidi mou.*"

"*Well,*" she countered, elbowing him as she did, "I only had the dregs to pick from at the tree lot, Captain."

"A good sailor's—"

"Ready for anything at any time." She rolled her eyes. "I know, Dad. I know."

"Can't say that Sami's cell phone shots lied about the outside, though." He swiveled the force of his gaze back to her. And by force, she meant a look that had surely served him well in prisoner interrogations. "Engaging in a little twinkle-twinkle therapy, sweetheart?"

She shrugged and turned for the kitchen. Anything to avoid his stare, which was cranked to the frequency of a piercing shot into her head. Shit, his scrutiny was like the bright-green version of—

No. Don't think of him. Not now. Not when Dad's watching for every change down to the sweat in your pores. Don't think of him, don't imagine him, don't remember his frittata right there on your stove or the way he backed you into that counter...

"I like lights, okay?" she managed to retort.

"Those aren't lights, daughter mine. Those are a fire hazard."

"You want a beer?"

"After you tell me who the hell he is."

Crap.

"What? He who?"

"Celina. Cut the *skata*."

The doorbell dinged, but Sami didn't wait for her to get to the door. Her niece came bounding in with a plate full of perfectly baked *Kourambiedes* and a potted poinsettia.

"Saved by the eleven-year-old on the holiday break buzz," Celina muttered. She waved to Dylan, who swaggered in after his daughter and, as usual, seemed to take up half the entryway. He looked especially formidable tonight, as he was still dressed in his camouflage work clothes and boots. His arms were filled with presents clearly wrapped by Sami, their seams lined in tape and a multitude of bows topping each package.

"Sorry for the grunge, Cel," he called. "Long-ass day."

"Yeah, yeah, likely story." The comeback came from behind him, with the distinctive dry drawl of the guy who occupied the birth order between her and Dyl. Sure enough, Nikola slipped inside, carrying himself with wildcat grace, still finger combing his navy reg haircut. Though just an inch or so shorter than Dylan, Nik always carried himself with an elegance that made him compensate for the difference. Even tonight, though he still wore camos from the waist down, he'd changed into a long-sleeved navy crewneck that accented his torso in all the right ways. Yep, Nikola was her sib with the smooth wardrobe and the smoother nerves. It had surprised no one that he applied for Explosive Ordnance Disposal training as soon as he was able.

"Hey, Versace boy." Dylan chuffed as he gave Nik a once-over. "Who the hell you trying to impress?"

Nik snorted. "It's Christmas Eve, assmunch. Did you even shower?"

"Hey!" Dyl jerked his head toward Sami. "Language, dick wad."

"Dear Lord," Celina mumbled.

"All right, you two." Dad issued the interjection. "Grab some beers and take it outside for a few." He reached inside the fridge and pulled out three of the bottles Celina always kept on hand for her brothers. But instead of keeping the third bottle for himself, he handed the trio over to her. "Your sister will be joining you."

Her nerves went on alert. Hell. She smelled a setup.

"Dad, I have a turkey *and* a ham in the oven."

"And now that I'm monitoring them, we know nothing will come out black."

Celina swung a glare at Sami. Her niece gave up a giggle. "Sorry, Auntie Cel. I couldn't help telling them about the cookies. It was funny!"

From the front door, Dylan yelled, "Get your ass out here, *kopelia mou*. Bring some of that flawlessly made *Kourambiedes* too. Gee, I wonder which awesome brother is responsible for that."

"Not funny, Dyl," she called back.

The snow they'd gotten on Thanksgiving had long since melted. Now it was just plain cold outside, making her glad for the beer's warmth in her blood as she joined Dylan on the front porch swing. She'd be even warmer if she were drinking some of Dante's Scotch—a thought that got banished as soon as it struck. Damn it, she wasn't going there. Not tonight. Not *ever*. She was better than that. She had to be. Mom and Natalie had let the beast suck them in. A few flashes of bling and a shiny sugar-daddy lollipop, and they were gone without a thought about the emotional destruction in their wake. She'd beaten the beast. She could sure as hell live without Dante Tieri's stupid expensive Scotch.

Living without Dante Tieri was another issue altogether.

"Crap almighty, Cel." Nikola stood on her lawn between a family of snowmen and a pair of reindeer that dipped their heads up and down, "feeding" on his boot. "Thank fuck I don't have to disarm *this* time bomb."

"I think you got that wrong, Fusion." Dylan wielded Nik's service call sign with an affectionate smirk. "Looks like the device has detonated already." He took another swig of his beer and stretched a hand around her shoulder. "The question is, *Celinitsa,* when are you gonna blow too?"

She surged to her feet. "Damn it, I knew it. Dad—"

"Is concerned about you, like we are." Nik barely moved as he said it, but his tone still struck like a slap. "You think because you're not hitting a front line that the rules of departure don't apply to you? Things at home need to be clean and right, or you're going to be worth shit to your country over there."

She turned on them, heading for the porch rail. She wished she could grip it, but it was wound tight with little glowing candy canes. "I'm fine, okay? Things are clean." Damn it, the "clean" was driving her crazy.

"What about right?"

The question came from Dylan. It made her shiver. He

never resorted to using a funeral-parlor murmur like that, unless he felt the situation was just as serious. Celina locked her teeth and gulped deep, fighting back the words she desperately wanted to give her brother, preferably in huge sobs against his rock-hard shoulder.

Right? No, Dyl. Things aren't right, because the only man who's made me feel more "right" in my life is fourteen years older than me, makes more in an hour than I do in a year, and turns me to applesauce by paddling my ass raw. I'm not sure how to make all that into a nice big case of "right," do you?

"I—I'm fine, you guys." She forced it out, knowing they wouldn't let up if she didn't.

"And reindeer really know how to fly," Nik countered.

Still using the funeral home voice, Dylan asked, "You want to tell us about him?"

She backhanded the tears off her cheeks. "No. Just—you guys—no, I don't." *I can't.*

What the hell could make this Christmas Eve more morose?

The next moment, she could've shot herself for the question. Dylan's cell, though set on vibrate in his pocket, buzzed into the night like a bomb fuse set afire. Celina turned and watched her brother's face as he looked at the screen. Correction: her brother's glower.

"Is it Natalie?" Her logic went there naturally. It would be just like Dyl's ex to call from some glamour port on the other side of the world, where it was Christmas Day already and she was celebrating with a sangria while some hunk named Hans gave her "stressed-out" shoulders a rubdown.

"No," Dylan snapped. "Worse." He rammed the phone to his ear as he said, "Kouris here, Commander."

Celina's stare locked to Nik's. "Now?" she whispered.

Her brother only shrugged.

Dylan got off the call fast. He didn't say anything as he repocketed the phone.

"What's up?" Nike asked. "You're not buggin', are you?"

Dylan's gaze, normally the shade of decadent chocolate, went thunder dark. "Yeah. I'm afraid so."

"What?" Celina slammed her beer on the deck table. "Aren't you supposed to be doing basic transports and shit now? Isn't that why you requested to be based here, mister single dad?"

"Sometimes situations call for duty in different ways, Cel."

Comprehension hit like all the lights on the house really did blow up. "Crap. *Crap.* These 'little hops' you've been doing... Oh Dyl, are you going on fighter runs again?"

Her brother looked down at the hand she gripped to his shoulder. Then raised his somber gaze to her face. "This isn't the time, Cel. There's shit happening that I can't tell you about. Let it rest."

"Let what rest?"

The question came from Dad, who'd opened the door and let out a tantalizing draft of roasted meats, fresh potatoes, and something with pumpkin in it.

"Damn," Dylan muttered. "That smells fucking good." He threw a fast glance at Dad. "Sorry, Captain. I'm not gonna be able to stay and enjoy it."

Dad nodded. "You do what you have to do, Lieutenant."

"Thanks, Dad. I will."

"*What?*"

The interruption burst from Sami this time. The girl

poked out from behind Dad, an iPod in her hand and new grief welling in her big dark eyes. "Daddy? What's happening?"

Dylan crouched down and reached for his daughter. "Samantha Karena," he said softly. "Come here." As his daughter rushed out and clutched him, using the seat he created for her with his thigh, he squeezed his eyes shut and kissed the top of her head. He enfolded her like she was a fifty-three-inch version of the Hope Diamond. Celina palmed back more tears, caught between wanting to embrace her brother in pride and knock him up the side of the head in fury. The dilemma only worsened when Sami's heavy sniff cut through the thick silence that had taken over the porch.

"Do you *have* to go, Dad?"

Dylan dipped his face into his daughter's hair for a long moment before speaking again. "Who are you?" he charged softly.

"Samantha Karena Kouris." The response wavered with tears.

"Again."

"Samantha. Karena. Kouris." She raised her head and said the syllables boldly this time. "The kid of the bad-ass, supersonic, bad-guy-whooping Falcon."

Everyone erupted in chuckles. "No coaching going on there, huh?" Nik quipped.

Sami was the first to go sober again. "I understand you need to go, Dad. But now who's gonna be my date for the Kris Kringle Ball tomorrow night?"

Celina looked up. Nik was already prepped with the don't-look-at-*me* scowl. Though attending the base's annual Christmas night bash was a family tradition, Nikolas made it a point to stay off the dance floor. Nobody ever argued. Nik's creator had given him the hands of a surgeon, the nerves of a Zen monk, and the dancing ability of a drunk monkey.

Thankfully, Dad spoke up. "I'll be proud to take you to the dance, *manari mou.*"

Sami but her lip. "Uhhh, no offense, *papou,* but...errr, you're my grandfather and..."

Dad chuckled. "I understand, honey. Your friends will be there. You want somebody with a hotness factor."

From the shadows just beyond the flare from the house lights, an easygoing baritone called out, "Will your new Navy SEAL uncle do?"

They all let out gasps of shock. The next second, a handsome, familiar face materialized from the darkness.

Dad got his voice back first. "Cam?"

Her little brother grinned and waggled his dark brows. He still wore his uniform. On the right side of his chest, there was a brand-new SEAL Team trident patch.

"Holy shit!" Nik was the closest to the street so got to his brother first. The whole family fast piled on top of their embrace. Celina gave up trying to hold in her tears.

"When...how..." She couldn't seem to form a full sentence.

Cameron laughed at her and looked up at the house in amazement. "Cel, I swear to God, I saw your house from the transport."

"Why didn't you tell us you were coming?" Dad broke in. "I could've picked you up, son."

"I didn't know myself until this morning," Cameron answered. "They put us through a crappy-ass morning PT and were waiting with the patches when we got back. Believe me, after that PT, the walk here from the 'L' was a jaunt in the fucking park."

"Hey!" Dylan cuffed Cam across the top of his head. "SEAL or not, watch your language around my kid."

"Eat me, asshat."

Nik chuffed. "Nice one, Cam."

Dylan barreled into both of them at once. The three men rolled across the lawn like bears fighting over a salmon.

"Ahhhh!" Celina screamed. "Watch out for the rein—"

Too late. The decorations got kicked out to the street.

Sami shook her head and planted her hands on her hips. "Jeez. Boys. They're never easy, are they, Auntie Cel?"

Celina curled Sami's head into the crook of her shoulder. Naturally, even thinking of answering the question filled her mind with Dante. She wondered what he was doing on this starry, chilly night. She wondered if he was spending the evening with all those people from the photos in his home, laughing and eating, or if he even tumbled across a lawn somewhere with his own brothers. Shockingly, she could really envision that. The image made her smile softly before she scraped it free from her mind and forced it to vanish.

"No," she finally answered her niece. "They're not easy, sweetie...but every once in a while, they can be worth the trouble."

CHAPTER SEVENTEEN

Dante thought about backing out of the Kris Kringle Ball gig this year. This would be his sixth return to the event; surely somebody else was chomping at the bit to get into the Santa suit for once. But Lois Stanbridge, the sweet little coordinator from the veterans' wives group that put on the party, had called and begged until her face was likely more blue than her hair. Just what was he supposed to use for a good back-out? He was out of town? A lie easily exposed. His puppy was crapping all over the condo? Not a lie but not effective; she'd just tell him to bring Star along with him.

For a wild moment, he considered the truth.

I'm sorry, Lois, old girl. You see, I'm barely in the holiday spirit this year because every other beat of my heart is screaming for a woman I can't have. Let me tell you about the night I gave my heart to her. It also happened to be the night she surrendered her body and spirit to me. Did I forget to mention the paddle and the anal plug I used on her? Did I also forget to mention there's a good chance she'll be at this damn ball?

Okay, maybe he'd be stretching with that last one. Celina had been dragged by her toenails to the Veteran's Day party, so what made him think she'd look on this bash any differently?

Because this was a family night, that was why. Because she had a niece whom she adored, who'd likely haul the whole family to the party. What kid on the base missed this thing? A post-Christmas bash where Santa made "one last stop" on his way back to the Pole? C'mon. No-brainer.

He started climbing into the padded suit that would turn him into the most popular guy at the party. He ran through a few practice "Ho ho hos" and jelly-belly laughs, but the Kringle vibe wasn't settling in yet.

"Get your shit together, Inferno." He zipped up the suit and started sweating, even though he wore nothing but boxers under the costume. "The chance you're even going to see her is one in five hundred—literally. It's not like she's going to *see* you in return."

"Oh, Mr. Tieri!" Lois Stanbridge's singsongy voice bounced up the stairs. "Or should I say, Oh, Mr. Kris Kringle! Are we ready for our grand entrance?"

"As ready as I'll ever be." He uttered the response to his reflection, pulling on the red velvet hat and forcing at least a small twinkle to his eyes. It was Christmas Day, after all. A little wish-granting magic was in order, even if he wasn't on Santa's "Good" list this year.

★ ★ ★

Two and a half hours later, his heart actually was lighter. The best and cheapest therapy on the planet was serving others, proven true to him every minute he spent with the excited base kids. A few even brought *him* gifts, including shared trinkets from their stockings and enough plates of cookies to keep "Santa" hefty for the next decade to come. He'd managed to relax a little too, when several scans of the room yielded no sign of a slender and graceful body, a waterfall of soft chestnut hair, and eyes that captivated like enchanted forests. Looked like the Kourises had skipped the bash. Thank God.

As the kids began to thin, a disc jockey plugged in and

started some low-key tunes to warm up the teens and adults for their part of the evening's fun. Dante got up from the ornate throne and made his way to the table where the cookie plates had been placed. He was hungry as a bear, and it all looked amazing.

He knew what he wanted as soon as he spied the powdered sugar mounds on the far side of the table. *Kourambiedes.* He'd gotten obsessed with the Greek Christmas cookies. The baked goods were a shitty substitute for the Greek "sweet" for which he was truly aching, to be sure, but he could think of worse comforts. Fortunately, exercise was also a compulsion when he was depressed.

He was about to pull the cellophane cover off the plate, when he lifted the flap of the note card taped to it instead. The message, scrawled in a kid's careful cursive, replaced the hunger in his gut with a mix of heartache, excitement, and urgency.

Dear Santa,

I hope you enjoy these Kourambiedes cookies. They are a Greek tradition at Christmastime. Beware! They are very messy, especially if you make them the right way—and my dad REALLY makes them good. His name is Dylan Kouris, and he is a bad-ass, supersonic, bad-guy-whooping pilot. He also had to leave on a mission last night. I miss him and I am sad ☹. But his cookies make me think of him, and I'm a little happier. I hope they make you happy too.

Love,
Samantha Karena Kouris
(Falcon's Daughter)

His throat was tight as he swallowed. As if the note now gave him the magical power to do so, he spotted Sami right away. She sat at a corner table with a few friends, all crowded around an iPad with some fast-moving game loaded onto it. Sami was giving the peer camaraderie a decent try, but it wasn't working. Her shoulders slumped, and her eyes kept wandering the room, as if some Christmas miracle would still happen and her father would appear.

Sitting at the other side of the round table was a younger officer in camos. Dante recognized him immediately from the pictures in Celina's place. He shared Celina's thick dark hair and easy smile. At the moment, he tossed his head back on a laugh from something the woman next to him had said.

That woman was Celina.

Hell. Just fucking hell.

"Stellina."

Over four weeks of separation should have gotten him over this, right? How could she still affect him like this, instantly seizing his senses, funneling his focus, possessing his every breath? She wasn't even dressed in formal uniform tonight, which only worsened the effect. The white cashmere sweater and the poured-onto-her-body jeans gave him instant ideas about jamming his hands under them, maybe in one of the deserted hallways around here. He'd kiss her raw and order her to come for him, as he pinched a nipple with one hand and her clit with the other...

"Damn," he muttered, looking down at the cookies again. "Damn it!"

Lois appeared next to him. "Mr. Tieri? Is everything all right?"

"Fine, Mrs. Stanbridge. Just fine." He flashed a

perfunctory smile. "I'm going to take a few more minutes, if you don't mind."

"Of course not."

He strode out of the room and back up to the little bathroom in which he'd changed his clothes. After whipping out his cell, he tapped in a quick message to Vincent.

Need the laptop from the trunk right away.
The big one. Thanks. D~

After hitting the Send key on that, he clicked to his contacts list. From there, he typed in an eleven-digit code that got him to a second secret list. After finding the name he wanted, he pressed the Call button without a second thought. Then he hoped like hell that the vice admiral was picking up his cell right now.

CHAPTER EIGHTEEN

"Hey, Sami. The DJ's starting to play some cool stuff. C'mon, girl."

Celina watched as Cameron rose and extended a hand to his niece. The grin he tagged on the end of his invitation made two out of Sami's three friends bust into enamored giggles. Sami gave a discomfited shrug. "No, thanks, Uncle Cam. Maybe a little later."

Nik got back to the table with another round of sodas and popcorn. "Hey, Cel. This bag has extra cheese salt on it. I know you like it that way."

She gave her brother a gentle smile. "You're the best. Thanks, Nik. I'm really stuffed from dinner, though."

"The dinner you ate three bites of?"

"You counted?"

"Last time I checked, I could count to three, yes."

Cameron shoved back in his chair. "Okay, what gives? Nik and I are trying to get at what's making you two girls morose as hull sludge, to the tune of being idiots about it. I only have forty-eight hours of leave, Cel. Do you and Miss Sami Sunshine want to give me a break?"

Celina punched her brother in the arm. "Cut Sami some slack, damn it. Her heart is aching."

Cam tilted his head and arched a brow. "And what's your excuse, Miss Three-Bites-All-Night?"

She dipped her gaze to her lap. And prayed for a convenient

Christmas interruption.

The DJ was *not* helping in that department. With timing that almost seemed to mock her, the guy threw a song into his mix that she hadn't heard since the Veteran's Day party. She knew this for a fact because it was the song playing when the path of her life collided with Dante's. When everything had changed in one inexplicable moment. When he'd seen into her, through her, determined to unveil her mysteries, no matter how scary the journey got for him.

"A spirit born of earth and water, fire flying from your hands..."

Elton John's lyrics filled the room and shone understanding into her soul.

"All I ever needed was the one, like freedom fields where wild horses run..."

"Oh God," she whispered. He'd gotten it from the beginning, hadn't he? He'd recognized their connection, their wild and beautiful field, from the start. He'd also realized how their Domination/submission dynamic made it all the better. Even that first night, in her bed...it wasn't just sex for him. It wasn't ever "just sex." It wasn't about labels, and yet that's what she'd plastered all over their relationship.

He'd looked at her and seen a star.

She'd looked at him and seen the guy with the checkbook.

She'd been so wrong. So narrow and terrible and wrong.

With a choke, she lurched to her feet. "I need to make a phone call. Right now."

Cameron gave her the Mister Spock brow again. "Is everything okay?"

"I don't know." Hell. Had she'd come to her senses too late? She remembered him when they'd kissed outside his building, standing barefoot in the snow with her hand pressed over his heart, but that had been a month ago. He'd been the city's most visible, unattached Christmas ambassador since then. And damn it, he even had a new puppy.

"Excuse me."

A smiling ensign suddenly stood at their table bearing a broad grin and a matching laptop. "I'm looking for Miss Samantha Kouris," he announced.

Sami pushed the iPad at one of her friends, her brown eyes huge and curious. "I—I'm Sami—uh, I mean Samantha. I'm her."

"Perfect," said the ensign. He set the laptop in front of her and then plugged it in and fired up the screen. He deftly clicked through a few windows until he got to a screen with the words Secure Video Line emblazoned across the top.

"What's going on?" Sami questioned.

"Merry Christmas," the ensign murmured. "Courtesy of Santa Claus."

Celina didn't know what unnerved her more: wondering what was going to happen on the screen or conjecturing why the party's resident Santa now scooted a little closer, watching them all with eyes she couldn't read. His mouth was carefully closed and nearly invisible under his bushy fake beard. She had no idea what to think about him—or the relentless scrutiny that really should've been creeping her out but didn't.

"*Daddy!*"

It took a full heartbeat for the word to register in her brain. "Daddy?" Celina echoed. She joined Nik and Cam in riveting their stares back on the laptop's screen.

Sure enough, there was Dylan's grinning and handsome face. "Sami?" he exclaimed. "Oh my God. *Paidaki mou...*you're the best thing I've seen all day!"

"Ditto, Papa mine!"

He was a little dusty, meaning he was indeed on some crazy secret mission that he *shouldn't* be on, but at the moment, the pure joy on Sami's face made Celina forget her irritation with him. She was numb with shock and speechless with joy, which made her glad for Nik's and Cam's presence. They discreetly asked Sami's friends to give her a few minutes alone with her dad.

Slowly, Celina turned her own attention back to Santa Claus.

As she took each step, Elton John kept singing about stars colliding and finding the one.

"I don't know how you made that happen," she said, "but thank you."

He didn't say a word. But she watched his throat constrict on a long swallow. The skin of his neck was the color of burnished copper...

Her stomach flipped over.

She narrowed her gaze, concentrating harder on his own. His eyes were as impenetrable as the deepest midnight...with tiny stars of dark purple.

Her heart halted.

She reached and pushed the white nylon beard back from his lips. And the very real, very black beard surrounding them.

He kissed her fingertip and whispered, "You're welcome, *stellina.*"

"Holy sh—"

He interrupted her with the mash of his lips over hers. And she let him. Oh God, how she let him. As her tongue submitted to him and her body ignited for him, thoughts were hard to pin down. Somewhere beyond the din of her senses, she heard Sami let out a squee and then proclaim to Dylan that Auntie Cel was making out with Santa Claus. Nik's and Cam's questioning grunts followed.

Reluctantly, she drew herself back from Dante. Still meeting his eyes, she said, "I'll be right back."

"No," he snapped and grabbed her hand. "I'm not letting you go again."

She smiled and squeezed his fingers. "Okay."

She walked back over to the open video chat, where Dylan peered out. She pointed to a couple of spots on the other side of Sami, indicating to Cam and Nik where she needed them to be. It was an ass-crazy place for a mini family meeting, but she was going to make it work.

"Well, brother..." She nodded down at Dylan. "Since you've clearly found it okay to take an unconventional route, so have I. Everyone please say hello to Dante Tieri. He's the one who arranged your little visit here with us today, Dyl. He also happens to be worth a bazillion dollars."

"*Cara,*" Dante muttered. "Maybe not a bazillion."

"Shush," she told him and then pivoted back to her brothers and Sami. "I also happen to be eyeballs-deep in love with him. You're going to need to deal with that. I know this won't be easy for you, or for that matter, for me in coping with you three. Dylan, in light of your special history with this kind of shit, I'm giving you a little more patience than the other two. Cam, Nik, I'm more than happy to answer the ten thousand questions you'll have, after I give Mr. Tieri *his* Christmas present."

"Gaaahhhh," Cam exclaimed. "Too much fucking information, Cel!"

"Hey!" Dylan yelled from the laptop. "Watch your damn mouth, SEAL boy."

She left them to hash it out as she pulled Dante out into the hallway. Once they were there, she laughed and jumped into his arms, kissing him again for everything she was worth. She stopped only to claw away his fake beard and then pressed her hands to both sides of his face. "I'm not letting you go again either, Sir."

"Good," Dante answered softly. He picked her up even past the bulk of the Santa suit and carried her up a flight of stairs into a small unoccupied bathroom. "Yeah, that's really good..." The lock banged into place beneath his twisting fingers, echoing against the tiles and drowning his moan as he took her lips again. Celina let him back her into the wall, loving how adorable he was in his frenzy to get himself out of his bulky costume.

"I'll try to get back over from Atsugi when I can, okay?" When she got a long chuckle from him at that, she frowned. "What? You're *happy* with just video chatting for the next six months?"

"No, *stellina.*" The last of the suit fell off his leg. He stood before her now in muscled, near-naked glory, his boxers doing nothing to hide what his body clearly desired for a Christmas treat. "I'm just damn glad I went ahead and ordered a deep cleaning on my Tokyo condo."

"What?" Joy rocketed through her as he put his hands to work on her clothes now. In less than a minute, her sweater and bra were gone. It took a couple more for him to slide the blue jeans completely off her legs. "So...what you're saying is—"

"You're not getting away from me this time."

He hiked her thighs around his as he positioned his face just inches from hers. He still didn't do anything with his boxers, sliding up and down to tease her clit and pussy with his silk-covered shaft.

"None of this is going to be easy, *stellina*. We're going to have issues. We're going to have bumps. We're going to have fights." A touch of mirth hit his face. "And God knows we're going to have your brothers and my mother. But I'm not giving up on us." He gave her an especially hard thrust as emphasis of that. "And I'm not letting you give up. Do you understand me?"

"Yes." She gasped and clutched his shoulders. Her head slammed against the wall as her vagina dripped and her clit quivered. "Oh God, Dante, you need to fuck me now!"

His beard scraped her skin with delicious roughness as he smiled against her neck. "Reach into my pants, on the counter. There's a condom in my wallet."

She got the foil packet out with frantic speed and then jammed a hand beneath his waistband, pulling out his long, pulsing length. "I love you," she said against his lips, rolling the sheath on for him.

His gaze glimmered with that gorgeous indigo sheen. He scanned every inch of her face with it before his lips curved in a passion-filled smile. "As I love you, my *stellina*."

As he filled her mouth with his tongue and her body with his cock, Celina opened one more part of herself to him. Her heart. Never again, she silently vowed to him, would she let labels, misconceptions, and the boundaries of others guide *her* soul. With his patience, his Dominance, and his love, Dante Tieri had set her free from it all.

She was really a star now.

And what a wonderful feeling it was.

ALSO BY ANGEL PAYNE

Suited for Sin:
Sing
Sigh
Submit

The Bolt Saga:
Bolt
Ignite
Pulse
Fuse
Surge
Light

Honor Bound:
Saved
Cuffed
Seduced
Wild
Wet
Hot
Masked
Mastered
Conquered
Ruled

Secrets of Stone Series:
No Prince Charming
No More Masquerade
No Perfect Princess
No Magic Moment
No Lucky Number
No Simple Sacrifice
No Broken Bond
No White Knight
No Longer Lost
No Curtian Call

Temptation Court:
Naughty Little Gift
Pretty Perfect Toy
Bold Beautiful Love

Cimarron Series:
Into His Dark
Into His Command
Into Her Fantasies

**For a full list of Angel's other titles,
visit her at AngelPayne.com**

He saved her life...she saved his soul.

Garrett Hawkins is the most valuable asset to his Special Forces unit, because, frankly, the guy doesn't care if he lives or dies anymore. Since the love of his life, Sage Weston, was kidnapped and killed with her medical unit a year ago, Garrett has turned the shell of his soul into the armor of a finely tuned fighting machine. Being the first tapped for the unit's craziest missions is just fine by him. The less time for memories and the agony they carve into his soul, the better.

It's a plan that works, until Garrett's world is upended one night in the jungles of Thailand. Memories become reality when the unit is called to rescue a group of kidnapped aid workers, and they discover Sage and her teammate among the retrieved women. Now that Sage is back in his arms, Garrett doesn't know what to do. He has changed in dramatic ways, especially in the darker tastes of his passion. If he touches Sage again, he'll want to claim her, restrain her...dominate her.

Is Sage's love strong enough to let Garrett back in, not only as her fiancé but her Dominant? Can she trust that visiting the new shadows of his life will lead her to ecstasy and not ruin? Or can Garrett's discipline be exactly what her soul needs to find its way back to life—and love—again?

Keep reading for an excerpt!

EXCERPT FROM
SAVED

BOOK ONE IN THE HONOR BOUND SERIES

CHAPTER ONE

Heaven.

He had to have died at last, and somehow—*God only knew how*—ended up beyond the pearly gates.

Garrett Hawkins didn't bother questioning the admission details beyond that. No sense in tempting Saint Peter, or whoever the fuck was standing watch today, into checking notes and realizing a mistake had been made. Wouldn't do the guy any good. At this point, Garrett wasn't past blowing the balls off anyone who told him he had to leave.

The deal was, heaven was nothing like the scene they'd taught him in summer Bible school. No sugar-spun clouds. No bad haircuts. Not a single angel with a half-tuned harp.

Heaven was silk sheets, his tongue on the inside of Sage Weston's left thigh—and her sigh in response.

"Garrett! Damn it! Higher. Please...higher!"

He chuckled and sank a soft bite into her tawny flesh. "Is that any way to talk in heaven, sugar? Ssshhh. You're gonna get us tossed out."

He spoke the last of it as he crossed to her other thigh,

making sure his mouth brushed over her glistening pussy in the process. Christ, how he wanted to stop there, and he thought about it as he watched new drops of arousal on her sweet pink folds, but there'd be time to return for all that sweet ambrosia and then some. In heaven, they finally had all the time they needed.

A shiver claimed the new skin that he began to suckle and lick. "Sergeant Hawkins, you're making me insane!"

"I hope so."

"Ohhhh! Bastard!"

"Mmmm. You taste like cream and honey."

"*Garrett!*"

He sighed and laughed again. "So impatient. So greedy." He trailed his lips toward her knee, inciting another protesting moan from the silk ribbons of her lips.

"Impatient? You've been teasing me like this forever!"

"And isn't it fun?"

"I hate you."

"No you don't."

"I'm leaving."

"No you aren't."

He was about to taunt the inside of her ankle when she really did yank it away from him. He raised his head in question, only to have the back of it bonked by her other foot as she swung that over the edge of the bed as well. "Sage! Hey!"

"Don't pull petulant on me, Garrett Hawkins. I invented it, and I do it way better than you."

He almost smiled. She'd been a ball of sass and fire since they'd met at that dive bar in Tacoma, and he loved her a little more every time she rekindled the attitude. It also helped him choose the next words out of his mouth, issued as a deep and heated growl.

"You're not going anywhere, Ms. Weston."

Her eyes widened, ablaze with bright peridot shock. She pushed out her chin and tacked on a smirk. "Is that so, Sergeant?" She stepped into a little white thong trimmed in sexy-as-hell pink lace and then tugged a white tank over the bra he hadn't gotten the chance to get off yet. "Why don't you watch me?"

He laughed, though the sound was made of anger, not mirth. Thanks to the countless sessions with Shrink Sally, as he'd affectionately come to call the poor woman assigned to "fix" him a year ago, he also recognized that the rage was directed at the guy in the mirror across the room, not the woman in front of him. That only tripled the resolve for his next action.

Without giving her any warning, Garrett hooked two fingers into the lace at her hip and pulled hard. The surge of her body returning to his side matched the rush of joy in his blood and the roar of arousal in his cock. This was where she belonged. This was so fucking right.

With a grunt, he twisted the panties tighter. The fabric gave way in his grip. It fell away, exposing her incredible golden hips. Sage gaped at him, though he took that from her too, ramming their lips together while he pulled her and flattened her to the bed again.

"I've got a better idea," he growled, rolling his hips so she felt every pounding inch of his erection. "Why don't *you* watch *me,* sugar?"

She did just that, jerking her brilliant green eyes wide as he jammed both her arms over her head and lashed them together using a bungee cord off his mission pack. For a second he wondered why his pack made it to heaven with him, but he was too grateful to question the issue for long. It was just as weird that her old bed had made it too, a wrought-iron thing he'd never liked much, thanks to its headboard full of fancy curlicues that tangled with each other like a damn tumbleweed. But right now he was really grateful for the thing. The two bungee hooks fit perfectly around a couple of whorls in the headboard.

With a frustrated whimper, Sage wrenched her arms. "Wh-What are you doing?" She craned her neck, exposing the nervous drum of her carotid artery. "Garrett, why—"

"I told you." He stated it with steeled calm. "I'm not letting you leave. It was a mistake to do that the first time. It was a mistake not to go after you. So now I'm keeping you right here, safe with me. Just trust me, my heart. You're going to be very happy." Without preamble, he tore her tank top down the middle. "And very satisfied."

Her breath caught on a sexy-as-hell hitch. "My hero." The sigh changed her voice, too. Her tone transformed from incensed to breathless but climbed into a strained cry when he took care of her front bra clasp with one deft snap. "Oh... mmmm!" she moaned, arching into the fingers he trailed around her dark berry nipples, pushing her puckered fruit up at him. He gave into the craving to sample one with deeper intent, pinching the nub and then pulling. Hard.

"Shit! Ohhh, Garrett!"

Damn. Her startled cry made him want to try it on the other nipple, and he did. Both her areolas were red and irritated now, their tiny bumps standing in attention around the distended peaks at their centers.

To his perplexity—to his shame—he got painfully hard.

That didn't stop him from getting greedy. With both his

hands on her tits now, he couldn't resist tugging on both her beautiful nipples at the same time.

"Damn it!" she screamed. "Garrett, th-that hurts! Oh God! Oh...mmmmm..."

She fell into an enraptured moan as he made up for the man-pig behavior, soothing each breast with long, tender licks. That wasn't a huge help to his aching body. His cock had gotten harder and hotter, throbbing between their stomachs. He shifted a little so he could dip his hand between her thighs, intending to continue his gratitude by giving her pussy a nice little rubdown—but what he discovered had him grinning in delighted shock. Her tunnel was gushing, warm, and creamy for him. She took one finger, then two, then three, her walls secreting more tangy juices all over his skin. Her arousal revved his mouth again. He pulled his tongue back from her nipple and bit into the stiff nub.

Her whole body bucked off the mattress. "Garrett! Hell! Why are you doing that?"

"Because you like it," he said while working a fourth finger into her. With one of his thighs, he shoved hard on the knee he'd just been worshipping, opening her legs wider. "Because the pain makes you wet for me."

He dragged his mouth against hers again, but this time she didn't let him into her wet heat. She opened her lips only enough to get her teeth into his bottom lip.

"Damn you to Hades," she whispered, her teeth still anchored in his flesh. He yanked back, licking at the flesh she'd torn open, though he did it on a dark smile.

"Too late, sugar. I think my passport's already got that stamp."

She looked adorable as she rolled her eyes. "Which is why

you're in heaven with me?"

Before he answered that, he did kiss her. He did it thoroughly and desperately, possessing her tongue in bold sweeps, permanently tangling his essence with hers.

"We've always lived on borrowed time, my heart. We both know it." He gripped her leg, hooking her knee around his shoulder. "Which is why I'm going to fuck you hard now. Which is why you're going to let me. Which is why you're going to love it."

Her eyes shimmered with tears. Her lips lifted in a misty smile. "Okay."

His penis surged against his fingers as he guided himself to her tight, glistening entrance. "Tell me you want it."

"I want it, baby." Her obedience didn't land him in heaven again. It made his whole heart and soul turn into paradise. "I want your hot cock, Garrett. Please. Now. Deep inside me."

"Yeah." He swirled the searing precome around his bulging head and then pushed himself into the first inch of her channel. "Oh yeah, sugar."

"Garrett." Her strident gasp filled him. "Garrett... Garrett..."

"Soon, my heart. Soon."

"Garrett! Fuck, man. Open the door!"

What the hell?

His fiancée suddenly sounded like his best friend. Correction—his demanding, door-pounding, subtle-as-a-linebacker *ex*-best friend.

"Hawkins! Get your ass out of bed and answer the door!"

Garrett slammed his eyes open. Squeezed them shut again. "No." His voice was a croak, absorbed by the grimy walls of the room in this no-name Bangkok hotel he'd checked into last night. He looked down, trying to piece together this new truth. The precome was real. One of his hands was still wet with the stuff. His fingers were also really wrapped around his aching boner as he lay beneath a mound of cheap, cloying sheets.

Sage was nowhere to be found.

Of course not.

Because she was dead. For a year, two months, sixteen days, and almost twenty-four hours now.

The knives of grief, all ten million of them, reburied in his chest. As he gulped through the resulting dearth of air, he raised his clean hand to his chest, scrabbling for his dog tags. More accurately, he searched for the gold band that hung on the chain between them.

Though his head ordered him not to do it, he slipped his ring finger back through the band. For one wonderful extra moment, the knives went away, and he relived the day he and Sage had picked out the jewelry... The day when he'd thought it would soon become a part of his wardrobe for good.

He remembered every detail of how beautiful she'd looked. It had been a brilliant late-spring day. Her hair was a cascade of light-brown sugar that earned her his favorite nickname, falling against the freckled shoulders that peeked from her pink sundress. But her smile... Ah, he remembered that the best. Her lips had glistened with her joyous tears and quavered with her soft whisper.

I can't wait until you get to wear it for good. I can't wait until you're all mine.

A month later, he'd gotten the phone call from Heidi Weston that upended his world forever. The woman who was preparing to become his mother-in-law stammered that he needed to come over right away. He'd actually packed a bag, thinking Sage had been hurt, maybe badly, judging by the sound of Heidi's voice. He was prepared to stay long enough to get as much info as he could about her condition and then head for the base to force himself onto whatever flight was headed anywhere near Botswana. When he'd walked in to see the Casualty Notifications Officer and the Chaplain sitting there, on either side of a sobbing Heidi, his knees hit the floor along with his pack. Only half their words had reached his brain through his roaring senses. *Tribal warfare...region unexpectedly unstable...van sidetracked off the main road... likely rebels...found burned out...nothing but ashes found...*

He swallowed hard and pulled his finger back out of the ring. As expected, his brain crowed while his heart screamed on the torture rack of memory. He waited, breathing hard, for the agony to end. He begged the wounds to bleed hard and fast, letting the anger get here and turn the pain into a scab. After that, he'd be able to move again. To function again.

"Hawk! Damn you, man!"

Anger moved in on the grief. Thank fuck. Fortunately, nothing got him more pissed off than Zeke's mommy-hen act. After rolling from the bed, he tugged on his briefs and then stumbled across the room. The dirty light and sound of traffic beyond the thin shutters told him it was about midday. Or maybe his growling stomach did.

"Okay, why are your panties in a wad?" He glanced at Zeke after opening the door, the last of his grogginess obliterated by the lime green and banana yellow print of his friend's tacky tourist ensemble. Z's khaki shorts were baggy on his timber-log legs, which marched him into the room before Garrett could even think about reclosing the portal. "Don't tell me you're bored, with all of Bangkok out there for the taking. We don't roll on this mission until nightfall. That gives you at least five hours to work your flogging arm and your kinky cock through a lot of cheap tail, my friend. I'll bet the girls at Club Subjugate are missing you something fierce, Sir Zekie."

"Sir Zekie. Aw. That's cute, honey." The guy kicked the door shut behind him. Zeke's six-foot-six frame was only a couple of inches taller than Garrett's, but the man's mountainous build intensified the effect of his stature, especially in this room seemingly designed for people half his size. "As much as Chelsea and Chyna like my side-by-side spanking special, shit like that gets boring by myself. You tried the fun-filled dungeon field trip once. Think you want to sign up this time?"

Garrett snorted and flopped on the bed again. His friend wasted his breath with the memory. Yeah, he'd gone. Yeah, he'd tried it. Z had gotten him in a weak spot around the six-month mark after Sage's death. He'd been desperate to forget the pain for a while, hoping "the magic of BDSM," as Z called it, would help. More urgently, he'd been hoping to figure out the kinky-minded demon that had been crawling in the back of his imagination since...well, he knew since when. The secret would go with him to his grave. An occasion, God willing, that would come sooner than later.

Needless to say, he'd scratched the itch just fine that night. Or, as truth would have it, hadn't scratched. That part wasn't such a state secret, and it justified the response he tossed at his friend.

"You really think that offer's relevant?"

Z shrugged. "Lots of water has passed under your bridge, dude. Maybe commanding a sweet little subbie will fire your rockets this time around."

"No," Garrett snapped, "it won't."

"Right. Because you'd rather stay here and just beat off after your wet dreams about Sage."

"Fuck off."

"It's been over a year, Hawk."

"Fuck *off.*"

"Fine." Z pulled the faded Yankees cap off his head, revealing the miniature broadcasting station literally sewn inside it, before scrubbing a hand through his tumbling dark-brown hair. "Turns out free time just got drastically cut, anyhow. That's why I'm here collecting your sorry ass."

He'd just cracked open a lukewarm soda and was about to take his first guzzle. He stopped the can halfway to his lips and shot a quizzical look across the room. "What do you mean, 'cut'?"

Zeke dropped into the room's sole chair and shrugged. "CENTCOMM received a line of new intel. Seems we're gonna be more effective going in to rescue these girls as the badass uniformed machines we've been trained to be instead of a bunch of American dorkgasms looking for some girl-next-door-type pussy." He stretched his tree trunk legs out, crossing them at the ankle on the foot of the bed. "So as soon as you get your ass dressed, we're buggin' back to the embassy. They're gonna let us change and get haircuts and shaves." He scratched the scruff on his jaw. "Thank all that's holy."

Garrett cracked a dry smirk. "You sure it's not just because you blew our cover with that shirt? Maybe somebody with half a brain looked at you and realized no normal person, even a dorkgasm, would willingly dress in that."

Z looked at his getup with a frown. "What's wrong with the shirt?"

"Oh c'mon. It's hideous. It's not yours, is it? Central gave it to you, right?"

"Yeah, uhhh, right."

Zeke followed up his hasty answer by cracking one of the shutters and feigning interest in the activity outside. Garrett rose, shoved into jeans and a plain white T-shirt, and listened to the scene that his friend beheld. Scooters zoomed, taxi drivers argued, bicycle bells dinged, and food sizzled. All in all, it was a typical day in Bangkok—probably the same kind of day that ten American aid workers had been enjoying just six weeks ago, prior to boarding a plane for their mission in Myanmar.

The five men and five women had never arrived for their flight. Two days later, the men had been returned unharmed, spelling out the abductors' purpose with more clarity than a Soi Cowboy titty-bar sign. Undercover CIA agents had been rapidly inserted on the case, and sure enough, after ample questions were asked and money was tossed around, they were invited in on the newest trend for discerning American businessmen looking for a good time in East Asia—American girls who would do everything a native girl would, at exactly the same price.

Tonight, the assholes running the racket were going to find a new surprise waiting for their sorry dicks. Garrett's blood surged with the anticipation of delivering that surprise. He hoisted his pack, slipped into his "lazy American tourist" loafers, and then cocked his head at Zeke.

"You gonna sit there moping because I called your shirt a fashion disaster? Come on, Fashion Sparkle Barbie. Let's depart this fair establishment."

To his perplexity, Zeke didn't budge. He closed the shutter

with unnerving calm. "Just another sec, Hawk."

The gnat of suspicion in his senses morphed into a mosquito. "What is it?"

"Sit down. There's one more thing we gotta discuss."

The mosquito started biting. "No," Garrett snapped, "there isn't."

Without looking back at Z, he went for the door and had his hand on the knob as his friend's rejoinder hit the air.

"You don't get to load up for the op unless we drill down on this."

Garrett watched his fingers go white around the knob. Officially he and Zeke were equal rank, but his friend's tone clearly pulled a top dog on him. That only meant one thing.

"Franzen put you up to this, didn't he?"

Z lowered his legs and then balanced his elbows on his knees. When he lifted his head, deep assessment defined his stare. Garrett almost rolled his eyes in return, but he caught sight of himself in the dusty mirror over the bureau. His hair, a nice gold when it was clean but the color of a worn dishrag now, was as rumpled and long as Zeke's brown waves. His eyes also looked like rags—blue ones that'd been used on muddy boots. His skin was sallow. He hadn't slept well in over a year, and it showed in every wrinkled, grungy inch of him.

He scowled. If he was Franz, he'd likely have a few concerns about adding his name to the mission roster too. It didn't matter that he'd proved himself on over three dozen ops in the last year. He knew the concern was for *this* trip. He didn't have to be told why. But he'd put up with the formality anyway.

"Yeah, okay," Zeke conceded. "The captain and I had a brief talk about your involvement on this one. You're a key piece of the team, Hawk. We could really use you. Even though you look like crap, your reflexes are still the best on the squad. You're able to make smart snap judgments even if the shit gets thick and the op goes sideways."

Garrett dropped his pack and leaned against the door. "Are you planning that much on this one taking a detour?"

"No. Hell, no." Like the protest about the shirt, his friend's answer flew out suspiciously fast. "It's just—we're gonna be deep in the forest on this one, G. I wouldn't be surprised if we come across fucking Jurassic Park or something."

"You know Jurassic Park is technically off the coast of Costa Rica and not Thailand, right?"

"It's sick that you know that."

"It's pathetic that you don't read."

His buddy's stubbled chin gave way to a grin. "And it's nice to see you getting pissy about something." In a murmur, he added, "Maybe there's hope for your humanity after all, Hawkins."

"Shut up and get to your point."

Zeke let the smile fall. "Okey dokey, Prince Charming." He rose and crossed his arms. "To be frank, the captain and I are concerned about your focus on this one."

A needle of irritation joined the knives in his chest. "That's never been an issue before."

"We've never been called to retrieve hostages before."

Garrett snorted. "Yeah, what about that? The Rangers and Delta getting their nails done or something?"

"You think I know or care? The op is what it is. More importantly, the hostages are what they are. American women, many with fair hair and eyes." Z leaned forward, intensifying his gaze. "I need to know you can keep the emo lockbox down on this, G. Complete objectivity. These girls will be terrified and traumatized, but our main objective is to get them to safety using any means necessary. The conditions will be shitty and the time frame will be worse. I need to know you can do that. I need to *know* you're gonna maintain your edge."

Garrett pushed off the door in order to take a determined stance. He bolted his stare into Zeke's, unwavering in his purpose, unblinking in his concentration.

"You think I'm gonna go cookie crumbs on you because some girl *looks* like her?" He shot out a bitter laugh. "You think that alone would do it? You really don't remember what Sage and I had, do you?"

"Why do I need to? You're doing the job to stellar perfection for me and half the world."

"And?"

Zeke's eyes slid shut and his mouth tightened, his version of contrition for the accusing words. "You haven't let go of her. You still got that goddamn ring hiding between your tags, which should be secured to your bootlaces, assface, *not* your sorry neck. I can write you up faster than—"

Garrett cut him off with a derisive laugh. "Oh, that would be entertaining."

"I've got genuine concerns here, Garrett."

"Got it, Oprah. Can I get you a tampon for that now?"

Zeke closed the space between them in one wide step. His jaw went harder beneath his stubble. "What you can do, damn it, is look me in the eye and swear to me that you're squared with the personal shit and are solid to go on this op."

Garrett notched back his shoulders and set his own jaw. He confronted the stare of his friend again. He'd seen those hazels oiled with booze, gunned with adrenaline, bleary with exhaustion, afire with exhilaration, and likely a thousand other things. But this was one look he always treated with respect. This was a stare of the guy who would be at his side out there in Jurassic Land, holding the gun that could save Garrett's life. He'd be counting on Garrett to do the exact same.

"I'm solid," he said. "And you know I'd tell you otherwise, Z." The last shrouds of his dream fell away from his mind, dissolved by the salvation of mental mission prep. "Let me help you get these dick lickers."

Zeke didn't answer at first. He subjected Garrett to another minute of silent scrutiny. That was all right. He'd been through it before. What he couldn't handle were the daggers Z kept trying to add to the others in his chest, to open up new parts of him so he could "move on" and "live again." That wasn't going to happen. Not today, not tonight, not anytime soon. The knives were his. The pain was his. As long as both were still there, he still had some part of her with him.

Finally, Zeke cracked a lopsided grin and chuckled. "All right, you charmer. Let's get the hell out of here. You need a shower, dude. Bad."

"Says the chump who smells like ass."

Zeke knuckled him in the shoulder. "You sure you got everything in that pack? Did you get your Jane Austen novel off the back of the toilet?"

"I've got your Jane Austen at the end of my dick."

"Hawkins, your dick is probably as blue as your balls by now." Z snapped his fingers. "Hey! Maybe that's where you should secure your tags, yeah?"

Garrett rolled his eyes, scooped up his pack again, and discreetly adjusted the body parts his friend had insulted with screaming accuracy. His cock was still doing its best to relax, though his balls throbbed in frustration, sending shots of erotic what-the-fucks at him. They were supposed to be enjoying some post-jackoff serenity right now, and the bastards were hitting the target damn well at reminding him of that every two seconds.

Get used to it, guys. He sent the dismal promise as he and Zeke made their way out into the sultry Bangkok afternoon. *Life isn't going to change anytime soon.*

ACKNOWLEDGMENTS

Special, unending gratitude from the bottom of my heart to my beautiful friend, Angela Barrett. You know the bazillion reasons why—always. Heart, devil, kissy.

A special shout-out to anyone and everyone stepping out to live your truth and letting yourself fly free.

BRAVA.

Embrace your weird.

Love the person that the Creator saw when he made unique and beautiful you.

ABOUT ANGEL PAYNE

USA Today bestselling romance author Angel Payne loves to focus on high-heat romance starring memorable alpha men and the women who love them. She has numerous book series to her credit, including the action-packed Bolt Saga and Honor Bound series, Secrets of Stone series (with Victoria Blue), the intertwined Cimarron and Temptation Court series, the Suited for Sin series, and the Lords of Sin historicals, as well as several standalone titles.

Angel is a native Southern Californian, leading to her love of being in the outdoors, where she often reads and writes. She still lives in Southern California with her soul-mate husband and beautiful daughter, to whom she is a proud cosplay/culture con mom. Her passions also include whisky tasting, shoe shopping, and travel.

Visit her at AngelPayne.com